THE
CONJURER

THE CONJURER

A NOVEL BY NICK OLIVERI

Write My Wrongs, LLC, P.O. Box 80781 Lansing, MI 48908
United States
www.writemywrongsediting.com
Copyright © 2021 Nicholas Oliveri

ISBN: 978-1-956932-05-8

To my parents (Fred and Kelli Oliveri), my aunt and uncle (Laura and Kevin Turner), and my grandmother (Judy Oliveri), my original and most supportive beta readers

To NAPH

To my friends in San Luis Obispo

To the Town of North Andover and its wonderful people

To the rest of the Oliveri, French, Turner, and Buckman families across the country

Chapter 1

Power is a dance of shadows.

Mikalla was the shadow puppeteer. In a way, Mikalla was the shadow himself.

The whole kingdom of Idaza gathered under the sacred light of the ceremonial flame, beneath the leather sandals of Mikalla, who looked down on the whole of the city from his platform with his crew. He was out of the audience's sight, high above and behind them. Mikalla, as the Conjurer, stood in front of the ceremonial flame, projecting his silhouette and his every movement for the masses to drink in. It was his shadow and his voice that permeated the eyes and ears of the audience. His body was the colossal shadow puppet projected onto Mount Chuxat, the giant rock formation that acted as the glowing orange screen for the countless commoners.

The commoners of Idaza were bound not by each other, but rather by their belief in the stories told to them. They were united in the blessed arcs Mikalla created with the flame and used to entrance them, week after week. Subconsciously, commoners needed a tether, a fabric—a careful, mythical lace that bound the legends of Idaza. The nobles had an answer for that, and it came in the form of the state-appointed Conjurer. The Conjurer's job was to make them believe. Belief kept the gears turning. The Conjurer projected the stories with shadows, and it was these legends that ruled the many hearts and minds of the kingdom. Mikalla's stories motivated every harvesting hand and inspired every nursing mother whose babies would grow up and swing hammers and swords for their kingdom with those same stories embedded in their blood and memory forever. In short, it was the stories and paintings in Mikalla's heart that kept the great kingdom running in beautiful unison—smoothly, peacefully, *collectively*.

At the end of every week, the Kingdom of Idaza gathered in the largest arena in the city for a ceremonial showing from the Conjurer and his crew. The forum was situated before Mount Chuxat in colossal, stadium-style benches, using the mountain's flat face as the projection rock. Giant shadows were cast onto the stone, depicting whatever the Conjurer dreamt up and created that week. Whatever tools the Conjurer needed were provided by the kingdom at a moment's notice. This included the symphony of instrumentalists Mikalla had at every ceremony, the props for the shadows, and whatever else was necessary to enrapture the hearts and minds of the kingdom.

The state saw the commoners as herded sheep. Mikalla, he was their shepherd. But Mikalla did not see it that way. In fact, Mikalla painted the pictures—of his heart, of his soul—in his most authentic way. That was all the nobles needed from him.

Mikalla created stories about the nation's gods (and the heroes, the lovers, the titanic villains), fantastic beings passed down to him through Idaza's mythos and the Conjurers before him. In turn, the government used their holy images—Mikalla's images—to collect harvest from the farmers, swords from the metalworkers, and so many more things that kept the kingdom turning. As a farmer produced food from the earth and the sun, Mikalla manufactured belief from stories and figures. Belief kept the kingdom turning; belief was like the sun in Idaza, energizing everything it touched.

It was a thin, delicate line that provided the mythical heart-tether to all things in Idaza: the unquestioned divinity of the position of the Conjurer—or the chief storyteller of the kingdom—coupled with Mikalla's primal, childlike need to create and portray stories.

The masses in the stadium seating below formed a sea of flickering, washed-out faces. Silence wafted through the air like a heavy fog as the shuffling feet on the benches and soft murmurs of the city's people waned to a hush. The cymbals blared and the gong boomed, signaling the start of the show. Mikalla gazed across the stadium from his elevated platform at the projection rock and saw his colossal shadow stare back at him—the same shadow the audience was glued to. He looked down at the sea of them like a god looked at his many creations. As he slowly and steadily waved his hand back and forth across his body, he saw their countless heads follow along with the rhythm of the shadow. Mikalla now had the delicious attention of Idaza in his grasp, and he intended to keep a tight grip.

He could tell the audience was transfixed when they swayed with him, unblinking and unwavering. It was then that he knew their wills were removed and replaced with his. The hundreds of thousands of souls within the arena were now united because they *wanted* to believe, and Mikalla made them.

After the cymbals clanged, he licked his lips and fixed his gaze on the eager audience. Every long second was silent. His arms spread wide, and his palms faced the black night sky. An exuberant grin crawled across Mikalla's face as he clutched the captivated audience with talons of iron. Although he walked on two legs and ate food like the rest, tonight, he was the sole enchanter who stood above the whole of it all. He was the caster of narrative whimsy, the *creator* of the gods.

Idaza's royal arena sat tens of thousands comfortably and could cram in the whole city when called upon, with the audience facing the flat slab of stone, the size of twelve elephants. Mikalla's crew were like extensions of his body as they painted their stories in shadow upon the projection rock. He and his crew worked tirelessly in front of the giant flame, shaping the shadow marionettes that danced on the rock to the whole kingdom below. Cymbals and drums collided to simulate pattering rain and clapping thunder. Despite the clear night sky and the dry desert air, the audience could nearly feel the drops wash over them and taste the mist. What looked like a comet blazed on the projection rock ahead. The voices of the kingdom's people bellowed all at once like an opera.

"Ahh oohhmm aahhhh ooouuhhh…"

Mikalla flicked and contorted his hands furiously in front of the flame and bit his lip. He had two crew members on either side of him fling chunks of dirt and debris into the air on his cue. One look at the platform, and it may have seemed like Mikalla and his crew were spasming. The projection rock told a different story. The flickering shadows on Mount Chuxat showed a blistering comet hit a rocky planet, followed by a crash and a deafening explosion. The audience let out one collective gasp. Mikalla closed his eyes at the audience's reaction and breathed in through his nose, as if to crystallize and inhale their excitement. He felt electricity flow through his veins, his arms, his eyes. Mikalla picked up a life-sized figure of a baby made of straw, cloth, and rocks and held it up in front of the light. Cast on the projection rock was the shadow of a perfectly alive infant—wiggling arms, grabbing fingers, and kicking feet. The cries of a newborn echoed and bounced all around the arena.

Mikalla filled his lungs with air and proceeded to speak. The words boomed out of his mouth, accompanied and propelled by the wind itself. "And Popoti was born. Behold! The bringer of

4

vitality and harvest for all Idaza. The rewarder of sweat and strife!"

In the same fashion and with the same precision, Mikalla continued to animate the life of Popoti, the God of Bountiful Harvest. The myth of Popoti was that he saved farmers and families alike from famine and rode giant eagles to survey the land. But that was not what solidified Popoti in the hearts and minds of the commoners. That was not enough to truly connect his feelings and his image. Mikalla's take was to show Popoti—though a sacred deity in Idazan lore—had flaws, too.

Mikalla was the chief storyteller, the Conjurer, for the entire kingdom. It was not enough for him to simply captivate the watchers—Mikalla had to leave them both changed and enchanted.

He entrenched his audience in the characters' lives. He swept them up in the torrent of the plot. And then, awash in the rapids of the story, he spat the audience out of the cyclone and left them transformed. They took away a vital piece of a larger existence from his stories—a portion of a greater consciousness. What Mikalla painted and played out all over the projection rock were the most human things told in the most grandiose of ways. Splayed out at every ceremony and coordinated with his acting crew was a giant, seductive reflection of all the people. When they watched the gods, the destroyers, the many warriors, and countless other characters during the ceremonies on the screen, they felt they were watching themselves. Pain, heartache, triumph—it was all there, thought up by Mikalla and amplified intimately in the hearts of the many.

That was the storytelling magic of Mikalla—it was his own bleeding heart that allowed for such a deep connection with the many watchers. He was simply the best to do it, the smoothest storyteller, and the greatest artist. He was meant to be the Conjurer.

***

Idaza was forged through war and bound by conflict. It stood as a commerce powerhouse in the middle of the Mesoas Valley, replete with renowned artisans, expansive agriculture, and strategic trade routes. Its primary export, though, was death at the tip of a spear. The hum of the seemingly balanced, prosperous city was supported by the graves of its enemies and dissidents. In Idaza, it was the indifferent gears of war that cultivated the city, and it was the hundreds of thousands of commoners that kept the gears turning.

But Mikalla, as perceptive as he was, didn't know the extent to which he was both needed and used by the government. His position and status in the kingdom were profound, and his influence was far-reaching; however, he always thought his ceremonies were for entertainment—not state control.

Chapter 2

"Well, Oro seemed to like it."

Mikalla glanced away from his gold-rimmed bathroom mirror toward his wife, Jani, whose thin eyebrows were slanted wryly. He always both craved and dreaded this part—when she would provide her judgment after his latest performance. "It was a very…" she continued, "*interesting* show, and certainly a different choice with Popoti."

"What? Did you not like him? How would you depict the God of Bountiful Harvest?" Mikalla said quickly. He always got defensive with his wife's criticism. No one could make him as overjoyed or as hurt as Jani could.

He stood over his tall, ivory sink in the gold-and-white-encrusted bathroom attached to his and Jani's master suite. He washed the dirt and ashes off his razor-sharp cheekbones and jawline and peered into his giant obsidian mirror. In Idaza, running water was reserved for nobility, most of whom lived in the small plot at the center of the kingdom known as the Inner Gardens, buried among spotless plazas and pristine parks.

"Well, couldn't you have made him… any *mightier*?" Jani chuckled and tossed her head back. Her brown eyes sparkled in the glow of the candlelight. "And could you not have made him any less *whiny* in the beginning? I mean, he is a *god*." She laced that word, "god," with irreverent venom, a mocking tone.

"I feel like he connected." Mikalla pouted like a wounded puppy. "You didn't like it, did you?"

"Oh, come on!" Jani caressed the back of Mikalla's neck with her slender, well-manicured hand. She wore gold bracelets and rings that matched her glittering earrings. "You saw the crowd. You had the whole kingdom captivated. Engaged. *Believing*. They drowned you in applause. Plus, I know King Oro was proud of you, too." She let out a sigh through her creased smile.

Mikalla clenched his jaw and stared into her deep brown eyes. "I could drown in a sea of applause, but without you, it'd still just be drowning."

Jani ran her fingers and nails up and down Mikalla's scalp. She had long, thick eyelashes she liked to use as weapons—never frivolously, always with a purpose.

She batted those eyelashes then. "Then you need to make something that deserves my applause."

Mikalla was taken aback—caressed in the gentle embrace of her hand and feeling choked by it at the same time. "W-What do you mean, Jani? What are you talking about—this didn't *deserve* it?"

Her long neck twisted and seemed to contort as her eyes circled and slithered around Mikalla's mouse-like ones. "I'm only kidding, Miki." Her smile was so sure and strong. It crept in all the right ways, every angle and movement of her lips perfectly crafted to meet Mikalla's fragile hopes. She manufactured a perfect laugh. It was a gentle flame that soothed the frost in his chest. "Don't be so hard on yourself."

"Yeah… it's just…"

"Just what?" Her hand stroked, her nails gently smoothing the rough patches and prickles on Mikalla's uneasy neck.

"Well, when you joke like that..."

Jani nodded like a parent to a child. Her assurance was golden to Mikalla's greedy needs. "I know. I know. But you need to know I'm joking." Another laugh trickled out of her curved, thin lips. It was a playful chuckle, but also heavy-handed, coaxing Mikalla to accept her verbal bandages.

"Okay... alright. But you liked it, didn't you?"

Jani looked away as they both walked into the bedroom, leaving Mikalla adrift, following along and staring into her sea of undulating, dark hair. It was that pause in Jani's speech that seized Mikalla's whole body. His breath locked up. Then, he perked up when Jani let out a long, drawn-out hum of thought as they both climbed into bed. Waiting. There was a whole universe inside Jani's pause for Mikalla—a gap of trauma and fortune.

"Yep," she said, turning over further so her back became a wall, "it was a fair job."

Later, after much silence in the room and darkness in their eyes, Mikalla inched closer to his wife. Deeper down than where the artist cared to look was a bubbling core of fear within him. It was a hot, melting place where many impressions of Jani resided—impressions of her apathy, of her cold shoulder, of her hollow gaze and her empty words. Somewhere between them all, connecting those impressions of his wife, was a truth Mikalla was unwilling to face. It was a pain he wasn't ready to carry on his shoulders, which weren't quite strong enough to bear the hurt of a whole lifetime's love. No, Mikalla never looked in the face of that icy reality—that he may be a tool, a means, a stepping stair to somewhere higher. The fear was always there under the thick layers of his heart, never addressed or recognized for what it was. That would prove too much for the artist. And so, Mikalla buried any questions of Jani's intentions as well as the whole weight of his worth behind the veneer of his art and the opaque blocks in his mind that held as steadfast gatekeepers to the annals of his winding soul.

Oh, Jani, a voice only audible to himself rang in his mind as he took in the dense, vaguely sweet aroma of her hair, *you love me so much you just don't know how to express it. You're scared to. But you love me. Your love is desperate, hidden, and heavy, but you love me. You love me like a bee loves a flower. I need you, Jani. I love you, sweet-haired princess, slender goddess. You're the light that pours out of my eyes. I listen to you, Jani. You must know that. Your opinion is gold to a greedy sailor, and Jani, I am that pirate that yearns for your luster. My princess, please be impressed with me. I'm sure you are. I'm sure you love my shows; you're just an astute critic, that's all. My Jani, and only mine, you love, love, love me.*

A rustle. A yawn. A hand surfed the quiet sheets. "Goodnight, Mikalla."

And with those two words from Jani, the poems in his head melted into primal action, an urge, a sweeping impulse. Mikalla poured and tightened himself around his wife. "Goodnight. I love you."

***

The morning sunlight streamed through the palatial windows just above the bed's headboard, drenching the bedroom in a golden glow. Mikalla heard little feet slap against the marble floor. A toddler with long black hair and deep brown eyes barreled through the doorway in his pajamas, dragging his stuffed lion on the ground.

"Daddy, Daddy!"

Mikalla scooped him up onto the bed and tossed him in the air a few times. Coyote burst out in a laughing hysteria, almost screaming.

"Okay, Coyotito, that's enough for now. You wouldn't wanna hurt Daddy!" Mikalla placed his son on Jani, who was next to him in the bed.

He put on his purple cloak gilded with intricate spirals and depictions of lions. Knowing he could walk into a room looking wholly different from even the most powerful noble fed his expressive spirit. It didn't make Mikalla any better. It made him different. His aversion to conformity was reflected in his constant polish, and, of course, things like embroidered lions and purple frills.

"When will you be back, Miki?" Jani asked, stretching and letting out a light morning groan under the thick white comforter.

"Shouldn't be long. I called a narrative review after my meeting, though. Would you mind telling the chefs to have dinner ready by dusk?"

After getting one last goodbye peck and taking another glance in the mirror, Mikalla stepped out from his marble floor onto the clean-cut cobblestones of the Inner Gardens. The colossal stone statue of Idaza's founding chieftain, Menizak the Great, towered in the middle of Mikalla's neighborhood, a circle of grand houses.

The giant sculpture stared into the green horizon beyond the city walls with his empty eyes set in a determined gaze, his body tense. One foot was cocked back in a fighting stance, and his arms were bent and flexed at his side. In his right hand, he gripped his spear, which was long and thinner than the handle of a pestle.

Mikalla continued walking. As his body rose with the sights and sounds of the morning, his heart sank back and dwelled on the night before. *Jani only had criticism.* He shuddered. *Why did she shrug when the others clapped? Is she jealous of me? How could a member of the royal family—especially one so beautiful— be jealous of me? Couldn't be. I'm sure she was just tired... But then, why has it been a pattern lately? I can't be imagining this behavior...* He smelled the air. It didn't carry the same rich, earthy taste it usually did.

Mikalla strode through the noble pavilion. He had an acute awareness of when others were watching him, and he felt that same instinct now. He straightened his back and puffed his chest, swinging his frilled purple arms in a proud pendulum. He came upon children he recognized as General Jax's kids playing a ball game in the grass.

"Great show last night! Praise Popoti!"

Mikalla smiled and laughed. "May he smile upon us this rainy season."

My image, Mikalla thought to himself as he strode by. The image that had come from nowhere except his own heart—his own mind's picture. Now, it was embedded into their souls. He thought it was marvelous. It's great what stories can do. I expanded their minds. I made them better... *It's great what I can do*. He continued striding by. His arms were like swings, and his chin levitated high.

Through a clearing in the royal pavilion, he came upon a stone wall so large it shaded the nearby shops. He walked along it until he came upon a wooden doorway twice the height of the wall and half as thick. It was engraved in gold with the words, *MAY IDAZA THRIVE FOREVER*. A small slit opened a few feet above Mikalla's head. A pair of eyes peered out at him, and within a few seconds, the slit closed with a thud. Elevated on either side of the giant gate were two stone platforms where two brawny men in black feathers, black linens, and with black-striped faces began yanking ropes the size of anacondas. They hauled in the rope without so much as a grunt or a bead of sweat, and the giant gate swung open.

Mikalla straightened up and took a large inhale as he stepped through the walls. In his path was a tall, statuesque man with slicked-back hair and reptilian eyes set in a gaunt face. His drooping cheeks sat just above his wormy-looking mustache, and pale, spidery fingers poked out of his black robes as they bid hello. The corners of his thin lips were pressed tightly and seemed to be held up by twine in a forced smirk.

"Good day, Mikall*a*." Kitan emphasized the last syllable of Mikalla's name when he spoke.

Why does he say it like that? This man is an enigma, purely contrived from the head down. What does he do to himself? Mikalla thought all these things and more as he bowed and greeted Secretary Kitan with the utmost respect. He wondered if his disdain for Kitan was noticeable to the secretary. He wondered if anyone in the vicinity could taste his oozing discomfort with the snakelike man.

"King Oro has been waiting," Kitan said, looking down at Mikalla.

Great. I'm about to get an earful.

They walked along the royal pathway made up of inlaid stripes of lush grass outlining squares of white granite. With every step Mikalla took, a jumpy feeling rose in his gut—a compulsive caution that made him both hyperaware and vaguely nauseous. Mikalla thought in pictures, and sometimes that unique perspective allowed him to see and feel things many others didn't. When he walked through the courtyard, he felt Kitan's essence— the aura around him—was shadowy, opaque. He couldn't get a clear picture of it, as he so often could with others.

Each blade of grass was perfectly trimmed throughout the royal yard. The king approved for the area to be stocked with gold fountains, stone statues, and tall, dark women in jeweled dresses. After a wordless race toward the royal palace, the pair came upon marbled steps wide enough to welcome a grand parade. Square pillars the size of sequoia trees with mosaic depictions of ancient battles rose from the floor to support the vaulted ceiling. Through the other side of the court was a lush clearing, complete with palm trees and a pool the size of a pond. King Oro sat facing away from the two with a jeweled goblet in his hand, laughing with a scantily clad woman in his lap.

Mikalla and Kitan knelt in the soft grass upon seeing the potbellied patriarch. Mikalla stifled a grimace as he bowed. He preferred reserving his bows for art or great talent—not simply because of worldly titles. He didn't understand why he had to lower himself before someone less talented than him. *Even a king must submit to great art. I'm on my knees with my head down in the grass... yet I'm what they all admire. I'm what they all need.* Mikalla peeked around and saw men in the same black garb he'd observed in the guard huts now surrounding the courtyard, surveying his every move.

"Your... Majesty," Kitan said as he bowed.

The king rose and turned, revealing his wide chest adorned with a vibrant shawl. He had a hardy belly, fleshy cheeks, and a broad, protruding brow. Although not a day over fifty, he had smile marks and deep forehead lines that creased his browned, leathery face. He stared at Mikalla. "You're late."

Mikalla's eyes bulged. He gulped and bowed, stuttering. Mikalla had command over beauty, yes, but the king had control over his position, his possessions, the spear, and nearly everything else. He had never seen Oro so coarse toward him.

As he walked barefoot over to them, the king's great gut trembled, and he suddenly doubled over with laughter, goblet still in hand. He stretched out his thick arms and embraced Mikalla with all his kingly might. "Ya know, that was a fantastic show last night, Miki. The people loved it!" His breath reeked of dry wine. "Kitan, you can leave us now."

Mikalla let out the faintest sigh of relief. *Oh, holy gods, I thought he was serious.*

Kitan knelt, bowed his head again, then left through one of the courtyard's many corridors. He signaled for two guards to follow him before slithering back into the shadows of the regal palace. The king grinned at Mikalla before taking his bearish hands off his shoulders. "Let's walk and talk, my friend. We have a lot to discuss."

Before they even took the first step inside the palace, Mikalla looked at his longtime friend, the man who was both dramatically above and below him at the same time. "So, you liked the ceremony last night?"

"Excellent." Oro escorted him with a phantom hand, continuing into the shadows amidst splotches of messy sunlight.

The pair arrived in a small room after trekking down stone spiral stairs jutting off from one of the pillared halls. Jugs and bottles peppered the many shelves along the wall. A resolute slab of oak lay on top of a tall wine barrel in the middle of the candlelit chamber, where they sat, facing one another. The king filled his own goblet and offered the wine to Mikalla.

"No, thank you... I haven't had breakfast yet."

"All the more reason to partake, my friend," the king said. Mikalla let out a soft chuckle and succumbed, pouring himself half a glass. After a few more minutes of small talk, the king drew a deep breath, tilted his head, and rested his closed knuckles on the table. "Do you know why you're here, Miki?"

Mikalla took a peck at his drink, leaned his head back, and inhaled. "Besides spending time with an old friend? No, I'm not quite sure." There was an unspoken dynamic between the two, with Oro having clear dominion over his friend, yet still holding a profound and primal connection to the man he'd known since early childhood. Oro had a unique and rare liking for Mikalla—the always-aloof boy who put his art above all. He was authentic and arrogant at the same time, and somehow untouchable, even for a king.

They'd met in school, way back when they had wide eyes and softer hearts—before the cold world had hardened them both. Mikalla was the only one of the schoolchildren who didn't fawn over Oro. The young prince was confused and enthralled by this—fascinated by Mikalla's rejection of the hierarchy, as well as the strong inner *life* that seemed to protect him from even the harshest externalities. A friend who didn't care Oro was a prince could also be a friend who cared Oro was a good person. The two shared this sensitivity—this unspoken bond over authenticity and a common affirmation of life.

"I know you're not one for foreign and economic policy." The king hiccupped. "So, let me put it this way. Our mines are doubling in production speed and output." He held his index finger down with his other hand as if reciting a list in his head. "Our farms are growing, and with them, hungry mouths to feed. Unfortunately," he hiccupped again, "most of our agriculture and mining are on the outskirts of our borders. Due to the rapid expansion of Idaza within the last decade, we are running thin on trained soldiers and had to stop our campaign in the east."

Mikalla held his face in a passive expression despite his amazement at Oro's sudden change in tone. The king's words jutted out, practiced and sterile, like he had rehearsed this speech. The artist felt a warm shiver; a darker, smokier aura trickled into the cellar room.

"*Apparently*, this has been a sign of weakness to neighboring states, and I now have reason to believe that…" The king scanned the ceiling as he paused. His voice got louder and more exasperated. "I have reason to believe that Chihopo is planning an invasion of large swaths of farmland situated on the north border."

Mikalla felt like an unassuming mouse caught in quick talons. "*What*? What about the treaty? They're really a problem? I thought we had peace."

"I thought so, too, but no longer." Oro cleared his throat and stared into Mikalla's eyes. "Do you have any idea what would happen to this kingdom if we lost those farmlands, Mikalla?"

Oh no, he used my full name. There was an air of nervous patience shrouding both men, but Mikalla could not quite grasp why.

"Do you know what would happen to our population? Our families?" In a shaky and deliberate theatrical display, Oro took his full goblet and dribbled a burgundy puddle onto the oak table just in front of Mikalla. The king clenched his fleshy jaw, eyes still locked onto Mikalla's. "Blood. Blood would happen. Everywhere." His tone was compulsive, and his eyes shook under his quivering brow. "I *need* you to set the record straight with the story you tell the people this week. I need you to *alienate* Chihopo and their wretched people." He slammed his hand on the table. "I need you to conjure hatred in the hearts and minds of Idaza toward Chihopo. They're enemies now, so make them out to be the terrible monsters they truly are. We'll need to recruit a vigorous force, and in order to do that, we'll need vigorous people." The king tightened his fist. "Light a fire that won't be extinguished, Miki."

"I... I'm not sure what you're asking me to do..." he trailed off, his voice too weak to trickle anywhere except Oro's anxious ear.

"I'm asking you to do what you've always done."

Mikalla nearly rose from his stool, but his calves and ankles refused to support his body. "But what I've always done is paint pictures and tell stories, and... reveal the human spirit. I make works of beauty with ugly scenes... but all in *earnest*. Earnest! This isn't authentic. This isn't earnest, Oro." The only thing on his body that moved with any deliberate weight was his head, shaking from side to side in scared, surprised disgust.

Oro stared at the ceiling, searching for more practiced words. "It's the same thing, Miki. But make the enemy Chihopo... their people... their king and their army." King Oro seemed to nod to a melody playing in his head, low, quiet, and slow.

"It's not art then, Your Majesty... it's a *contrivance*! You're asking me to *lie*? With my craft?"

The king's bottom lip tightened and grew under his flaring nostrils.

Mikalla's gut sank. His legs trembled, his vision spinning as he considered what King Oro was asking him to do. In a handful of minutes, he had gone from artisan to mercenary, high architect to builder, creator to pusher, publisher to *propagandist*. Mikalla constricted his body so his anxiety spurted out of him in short, jerky motions. Since it would be unwise to express himself any further, he had to subdue the visceral reaction pleading to be released from his body. Silence spread between the two. It was a passing storm both quiet and loud. Oro cleared his throat.

Though the room was warm, Mikalla began to shiver.

The king raised his eyebrows and dropped his mouth. "I'm not waiting for a reply, Mikalla. I'll be looking forward to the next ceremony… You'll be escorted out now." Oro swayed to one foot as he dismounted his chair and stumbled backward slightly.

The two ascended back up the stone spiral staircase toward the light of what was now midday. *Why do I have to walk in line right now, in stride and up the stairs? I want to walk where I wish, not where I'm forced to.*

Every stair climbed pricked a pin in Mikalla's ease; every moment of silence between him and the king felt like yet another chain that clung to his soul.

The empathetic king had a dissonant authority about him. In a way, he was just as oppressed as Mikalla—his friend's craft was being impeded, squashed, corrupted by politics. The conflict within him was palpable, and his disappointment in having to give this command to Mikalla hurt him. He just had to refrain from showing his hurt.

But the wash of the burgundy elixir silenced his eager nerves; the smooth burn in the back of his throat numbed the guilt of stepping on Mikalla's toes. The viscous, kingly potion helped him see his friend in a straightforward way, with a less personal edge: He may be an artist, a performer, and a friend, but after the maroon liquor sank in, he was just a man who had a job to do—just like the rest of the kingdom during wartime. *He has a rather important job, though*, Oro thought.

Chapter 3

Mikalla hated the decadence of the aristocracy. Born into the lower nobility of Idaza, he was the son of two government clerks and was exposed to the finer things in life from a young age. He pitied those who indulged only for indulgence's sake. Yet, that was a fault he saw his wealthier peers succumb to so often. As an adolescent, he had inspected his school friends' giant estates filled with fine pieces of art that were seldom glanced at, classic literature that collected dust on thick mahogany shelves, and antique imports annexed to obscure parlors rarely visited.

The same nobility who indulged in rich foods and rode around cities in glistening caravans were the same people who waged war on the backs of peasants and unswept ghettos. And war, to Mikalla, meant all the ugliness life had to offer—a denial of humanity at its core.

Oro's thick face still hung in the cellared shadows of his mind whenever he blinked. Those grim eyes, *that grim order*. Mikalla shuddered. Once again, a noble with more than him impeded on his life, shoved a rusty wrench in his affairs, and tried to contort his art to his own end—to the artist who gave everything to his craft, that was the ultimate indignation. But there was a glint, a chink, a slight hitch in Oro's delivery that made Mikalla think there was something hidden—some rummaging rat under the carpet, gnawing on the vital strings of power in Idaza.

To Mikalla, most of the nobility were satiated to the point of apathy; their senses were dulled by excess and self-importance. He buried his opinions deep within himself, though. He couldn't escape his own perceptions, nor could he escape the person he was, so he hid himself in angsty displays of standoffish pomposity and shy pretensions. From a distance, Mikalla was a flash of blistering color, more like a walking lightning bolt than a mere human. The closer one got, the more the intricacies of every sequin, stripe, tassel, and feather came into focus. Mikalla was grandiose but sensitive—flamboyant, but under it all, *delicate*.

Everything that oozed from his pores and shot out of his mouth was but a flicker from the sharp flame within him. It was a wild, animalistic compulsion, an urgent need to have his insights and emotions fly from his heart and onto a page, or a screen, or shadows on a rock. This contrived task—this warmongering, brutish job—handed to Mikalla directly opposed that instinct within him.

Mikalla's parents loved him for his perceptive, contemplative nature. King Oro (Prince Oro, when they met) loved him because he never gawked at his power nor treated him like anything else but a human. Jani loved him because he loved *her*, and he constantly strove to meet the impossibly high bar she measured his career with.

To Mikalla, life could be beautiful for everyone, and to ignore, deny, or impose upon that fact was a high crime in his book. He had a harsh flame within him that had the capacity to singe and burn and bring cities to heaps of ash if left unchecked. All he wanted to do with that flame, though, was illuminate the murals on the walls in the dark labyrinth of life.

***

Mikalla tried to stay as discreet as possible whenever he ventured into the city commons, but all too often, he couldn't help but stand out. He *needed* to stand out—it was that same animal compulsion that beckoned his bleeding heart to create, that childish urge he never quite grew out of. But this time, he strove to be inconspicuous. At the entryway to the common realm of the masses of Idaza, he stopped at the guard annex to hydrate and borrow a plain brown cloak to conceal himself. He adjusted his wide hood and took off for the Idaza commons.

The most noticeable aspect of the commons was the noise pollution that pervaded the air. Although it was made up of beckoning merchants, stern parents, guards giving chase, elders chatting over tea, basket weaving, stew churning, children laughing, maize grinding, and much more, it all mixed into a muffled cacophony that sounded more like static than any one particular sound. Mikalla had come to know the vibration of the city, the beat of its heart, and the movement of its vital blood. Most streets were wide enough to allow for the passage of cart peddlers and pack mules, but little else. Thin canals crisscrossed throughout the entire city, making way for recreational rowers and petty cargo transport. Every third person seemed to be carrying a wide maize basket or a brimming water vase overhead. He stopped to marvel at the steady vibrations of the bustle as he eyed the nearest artisan shop and shimmied his way through the determined flow of passersby.

The entryway to the artisan shop was supported by two long sticks holding the tent canvas apart on each side. Mikalla ducked into the tent and kept his hood low to shroud the top half of his face. He saw painted depictions of laborers and skinny children playing ball games. He bent over to inspect a stocky striped pot.

It was a seductive composition of violet, scarlet, and beige, and upon a closer look, he could tell by the grain of the clay and the pressed prints that its creator had toiled over it—most likely for hours to days at a time.

A small smile crept over his face as he envisioned the potter, alone in the back room of her family's modest shanty with the indifference of the city filtering in through the window and the incessant clank of her husband's hammer. Still, she worked. Instead of grinding maize, tending the garden, or assisting in the ironwork, she sculpted the pot from the vision she held in her mind and the small cut within her soul that could only be bandaged by her creative expression. And this expression—this divine creative will within the peasant artist—was about to be taxed and quashed for some fruitless war against a poor, dry city. The measly proceeds from that woman's handiwork were about to be taken to make a spear or a club for a fruitless war. Mikalla had a vision of an innocent street child in Chihopo being mutilated from the profits of this pot, and because of the strength of the story he was tasked with telling. All this surged through his mind while he stood in the shop.

"How much for this one?"

The shopkeeper, a hunchbacked old man who wore a hardy smile and an off-white robe, replied, "Twenty-five cacao."

Mikalla, with the pot tucked under his arm, laid a thumbnail-sized chunk of gold on the splintery table, gave a curt nod, and left, an easy smile still on his face.

"Th-thank you!" The old man's voice was tired and toothless, but—for that moment—exuberant. He scampered to peek his head outside the tent to catch another glimpse of the generous, hooded stranger. But it was too late. Mikalla had disappeared into the bustle of the streets, pot tucked under his arm, with determined swiftness in every stride away from the artisan's shop.

He bought a clay pot, but what he paid for was its essence. He saw a vital life force in that object, imbued with power, strength, and struggle. He saw that pot for what it was, not for what it looked like. He saw the city for what it was, not for what it looked like. *I just can't take from these people. I can't take from these families. I want to help them, not trick them! When was the last time Oro went to the commons, drank from the public fountain, saw a child nibbling old bread while being stepped over?*

While maneuvering through the bustle, Mikalla saw souls, people, *beings*—not just a collective crowd. These were the people he was commanded to sacrifice. The ones who wore plain robes every day, the ones who made pots with their whole soul, and the ones who constructed the stores to sell them—the builders, the artisans, the farmers, the workers. *Oro is commanding me to bring these people to the slaughter—to lie so we can impoverish the poor even further. The king drinks wine, and the general eats fat duck all day. And yet, they want me to take money from the woman who pours her being into a simple pot—an art that is her only solace from the dust and the hunger? Nonsense.*

Her life matters. The clay shaped by her tired hand matters. I refuse to throw her into the abyss.

Chapter 4

The secretary sighed and looked around at the kingdom—every pathway, an opportunity; every passing pedestrian, a means to an end. *But then again*, Kitan thought, *how could I not look at people as tools when they display such easy levers—open and awaiting my grasp?*

Kitan walked on through the gardens. Whenever the secretary went anywhere, he always scanned the landscape. He surveyed every nook he passed and took note of every face he saw—how they contorted and smiled and expressed. Faces, to Kitan, were mirrors to the soul. Tools. When Kitan looked at buildings and mountains and markets, he saw them for what they could be, not just for what they were. When he looked at a government—or a leader such as Oro—he saw it for its possibilities, its potential. But sometimes, this vision of his led him to act as a harsh critic, while at others, it spurred him to action—into the shadows to maneuver, plan, and organize. He had many pieces in his puzzle, and the Kingdom of Idaza was just one of them.

The shadiest meetings sometimes take place with the brightest of views. The view from General Jax's balcony overlooked the Inner Gardens, the whole city commons, and even stretched beyond the outskirts of Idaza's agricultural district. The rolling plains and misted mountains were breathtaking to most, but all they were to Jax were plots on a political map. The decorated general had a square jaw, hard gray eyes, and a prominent brow. Whether his hands were in his lap or behind his back, they always seemed to be clasped together—clenched and ready. He wore long, sharp-shouldered, red and black robes made from thick, heavy cotton. Secretary Kitan sat in the wicker chair opposite him at the circular coffee table overlooking the view, with both their backs to Jax's manor.

In his weathered, raspy voice, Jax asked, "And Oro—what does he know of this?"

"Oro? *Ha*!" Kitan spat. "Oro is a drunk and a barbarian. He *knows* what I tell him." Kitan crossed his legs and scanned the vast scenery. "And *you* know what I told you." A rare tinge of disdain tainted Kitan's tone, an emotion of his that seldom reared its head in public. As a true pragmatist, even Kitan's outbursts were calculated. Knowing General Jax and having very little respect for his intellect, Kitan knew he could get by with more slipups around him with fewer consequences. He was, after all, pulling many nuanced strings of political power, and General Jax was the easiest string to pull.

Jax grunted and stroked his chin. His hard, empty eyes scanned the horizon. From his vantage point on the deck, the commoners were ants. The lively bustle of the city's heartbeat couldn't be heard from the general's refuge. "Okay, then. I'll ready the barracks."

Kitan leaned in with his eyebrows raised and one hand on his bony chest. "Very well. I'll be sending a diplomat to Chihopo's capital in a last-ditch effort to restore peace. If and when that fails,

I will count on you to strike with the tenacity of a thousand suns. The future generations of Idaza will *revere* you, General. You truly are our greatest asset in this fight," Kitan said. His thin lips formed a worm of a smirk, and his reptilian eyes widened, if only for a moment.

***

It was not in Kitan's nature to show excitement or disdain the way he did with the general that day; his amorphous face was almost always calibrated to his situation and not his internal feelings. What *was* in Kitan's nature was the ability to know when a milestone was reached. With General Jax in place, the secretary couldn't help but show excitement at being one step closer to his vision—his grandest vision, the one that would make his life of maneuvering and sacrifice worth it. As pragmatic as Kitan was in his daily means of execution, he had an inner drive that was starry-eyed and childlike. The visionary side of him held a fiery contempt for incompetence at high levels. He had the foresight to see how much better things *could* be paired with the ability to see things for what they truly *were*.

To Kitan, Idaza was lost to negligence. It was an unsalvageable travesty he couldn't forgive King Oro for. Instead of overtaking Idaza, Kitan's long-term ideal was to connect it, to mobilize it, and to *transcend* it.

A smile rolled over Kitan's face like a wave. *All in due time*, he thought to himself. And then another image, smaller yet nagging, plagued his thoughts: Mikalla. Mikalla the fairy, the "free spirit," the one always outside the lines. *Everyone else is easy*, Kitan thought. But that flamboyant, flighty artist—to Kitan, there was no rationale inside that one. No logic to be had. He decided to keep a close eye on the one who stuck out the most— Mikalla.

The divine *Conjurer, the useless deviant*, Kitan fumed. *A man whose only value derived from his distinction from the norm. But*

I will have him cornered in due time. I will have all of them cornered in due time.

Chapter 5

The Conjurer would do anything to stay true to his work. The rest of the nobility didn't understand Mikalla's art all that well, and he decided to use that to his advantage when constructing his narrative.

Mikalla placed the striped pot in a corner of his study, sat down, and drew a deep breath. His new pot's luminescent powers gave the room a gentle glow in Mikalla's eyes. Having a collection of things so beautiful, cared for, and toiled over was a luxury that crept into his heart and nuzzled into its warmth; it was fine medicine for a sensitive soul. His study was situated on the top floor of his home, tucked away in a nook where he could block out the commotion of the servants preparing dinner, Coyote's homeschooling, Jani's meetings, and any other happenings in the house. It was a haven, a studio, a gallery littered all over with the things of low people with high minds, bleeding hearts, and shabby hands. Power. *This is power and life—all the abundance of culture and influence I need, right in this room*, Mikalla thought to himself.

The window in the corner of his study revealed a direct view of Menizak's statue. Mikalla squinted out of the lone window of his office, examining the statue. Menizak the Great was depicted wearing soldier-grade, double-stitched leather sandals and holding his trusty spear. His Achilles tendons looked sharp and bouncy, and they supported toned calves that could leap and sprint and kick. Chieftain Menizak had an athletic build and broad chest. Every fiber of his being was primed to face the enemy. Menizak the Great, in his deified stone depiction, was less of a warrior and more of a machine of war. The whole of his life experience, whether training, hunting, playing, seducing, building, studying, or praying, was all built upon the foundation of the razor-sharp spear he gripped and the number of people he had buried its silver point into.

Mikalla realized that Idaza, too, was built upon that same spear, and today, Mikalla himself had been commanded to fuel the war-making myth this weapon embodied. Yes, he'd depicted violence before. Yes, he'd depicted great wars, too, with bloodshed enough to fill an ocean. What he was being asked to do, though, was incite one himself. He was commanded to be the cause of the bloodshed, the taxation, and the collective draft of the many common people. He was to be the spark that provoked the very real hellscape of war—in real life and flesh. *This* he could not stand for. This he could not execute in real life. It may have been the Idazan way, the Idazan history, but it was not *his* way.

Regardless of how friendly—or intoxicated—King Oro was, he was still the king, and there was a certain finality to everything he decided. A royal decree was a command, and it was as serious as life itself, even to someone as high-ranking as Mikalla. However, inciting and spreading hatred gave him a visceral unease. Ceremony after ceremony, he reveled in having the weight of the kingdom on his shoulders, and now with that weight, he was commanded to weave a tale that would lead to certain death—massacres and mutilations of the same flesh that could paint and carve and write. He was to be the sun that would ripen the crowd for carving skin instead of wooden ornaments.

Knowing he had to sell a war to the people of Idaza made him sweat, made every muscle tense. He feared for the world Coyote would grow up in. The infants in Chihopo who didn't get stabbed or burned would certainly be held in bondage or taken for sacrifices. Heads would be strewn about, all over some land. *Why can't a diplomat solve this?*

Steeped in inner conflict, Mikalla turned his tense face toward the mural in his study. It depicted the gods of Idaza he so often included in his stories. He'd commissioned a street artisan to paint the frenzied scene; some of the gods were feasting and laughing, others fighting and competing, and still others having sex and groping. To Mikalla, this irreverence toward the gods was not out of defiance, but rather his own realistic views and goals: He saw moral value in deriving lessons and beauty from their all-too-human escapades rather than dogma or tradition for its own sake. Of course, if he wanted to, Mikalla could portray the gods as flawless and pure, but all that would do was propagate conformity and, almost worse, *boredom*—two things in people and society as a whole that gave him a sickly feeling. However flawed the gods of Idaza may have been, he wished he could call upon some of their awesome power and cunning right now in his suffocating moral predicament.

After a few more anxious minutes of scanning the mural and chipping away at his fingernails, he got it. The answer came to him like a divine, devious gift bestowed by beings too powerful to care about consequence and too bored to watch over a world without conflict. He *had* to tell the story of Chihopo as commanded by the king, but he did not have to tell it *well*.

He shot up, grabbed the jagged stack of amate paper out of his desk, then started off toward the royal studio to meet with his crew, his head held high and a bounce in his step.

***

Mikalla treated his crew with leniency and compassion. In return, they gave him loyalty, respect, and a keen dedication to his goals. Because of this, they were normally in good spirits and happy to await direction from him. When he strode in, though, he felt a certain sullenness dimming the studio. He found the crew—actors, musicians, and all—gathered in front of the studio's theater rock in a messy circle. As he approached, he saw many perplexed faces—twisted brows, bitten lips, stroked beards, and the like—but also one unfamiliar face.

A mousy, middle-aged man with a clean robe and a stony half smile stood among them. He held parchment and an inkwell with two hands and somehow made them look heavy.

"Hello, Mikalla. I was sent by the royal court to oversee this week's story ceremony." He had a rhythm to how he spoke. "I'm an official here to monitor your narrative process and verify your method of communicating our most urgent message of tribal defense. I believe you were briefed by His Majesty today, so I'll let you handle it."

Mikalla looked as if he'd seen a ghost. He felt like it, too. His plans of "accidentally" bungling his message to the people had just met a very bureaucratic hurdle—an annoying, scrutinous eye that he had to learn more about.

Mikalla spared all manners and decorum with the mystery man. "Who *are* you?" he asked.

The clean-cut official was taken aback. "Ahem. My deepest apologies, sir. My name is Zacatilanzec, but you may just call me Zac." He lost the rhythm he'd spoken with earlier. "I was sent by the royal court to ensure there are no discrepancies in the message you're sending to the public."

Mikalla understood. He was there to spy on him. Zac was there to make sure Mikalla compromised his art in every way possible before he compromised the state's message of declaring war on Chihopo. He figured it was Oro who had sent Zac and left it at that in his head. He had enough to deal with already, and delving into a political rabbit hole would only impede him from navigating his job.

He surveyed the faces of his crew. They looked like they had stepped into a portal that had dropped them in a backward, alien world. Mikalla had to play it safe, at least for now.

"Okay, everyone, we have a job to do and an outline to flesh out. This week is going to be a realistic piece set in the present day, reflecting some current events. Themes will include courage, collective sacrifice, and... *deception*."

Zac sat in one of the many empty audience seats. While still watching the crew stand staggered from one another with their hands on their hips, he began to organize his papers on his lap and set the inkwell on the arm of the chair. The crew, Mikalla included, watched him do this, and no one said a word. There was head-scratching, lip-licking, and foot-tapping, but no words exchanged between anyone for what seemed like hours. The only sounds in the studio were the scratch of Zac's pen and the occasional clearing of his throat.

Mikalla spoke up, "Okay, everyone, we'll have a break. Take a moment to reflect and prepare. I'll be in the courtyard if anyone needs me."

He turned to leave before he finished the sentence and strode briskly toward the nearest exit. The city allocated little land for the studio, but it had a petite garden in its courtyard with ripe fruit and white blossoms on the ground.

Mikalla ran his hands down his face and turned in place. He saw one of his drummers, Doz, had followed him. Doz was one of the few people in all Idaza who lived in the city commons and got to enter the Inner Gardens. He had a round face and soft eyes that were often circled by dark, puffy bags, and he had a soft voice that he mainly used on his children. When he picked up the mallets and started playing, the percussion reverberated a pain that Mikalla felt with every stroke. Mikalla called him the Onion because he made his drum cry, but that was really Mikalla's way of blunting the way Doz made him feel when he played by slapping a label on it. There were no concrete words that could correctly capture the emotion that struck the room when he put sticks to skin, other than it was transformative and enchanting, and Mikalla had to keep him around to spread his gift to the people—even if he was a commoner.

"Excuse me, sir," Doz said.

"Hello, Dee. What seems to be the problem?" Mikalla said, his voice cracking a little. He was now hunched over on a bench in the studio courtyard, looking like he'd just run a race.

"Well, Mikalla, some of us were talking…" he trailed off for a cool, meandering second, "and we feel like—"

"Gentlemen," a proper, snide voice called from the courtyard entrance.

It was Zac.

"Hey Doz, you mind giving us a moment?" Mikalla said. The confused drummer turned around and walked back inside the studio. Zac passed right by Doz without so much as a glance the commoner's way.

"Everything alright, Mikalla? Is there a problem? You know, if I—"

"Look, I'm sorry to cut you off. I think the reason I'm at a little bit of a loss here is, well, to be honest… I desperately want to serve this kingdom to the best of my abilities. With that said, I am *so* bent on making sure I do a good job, I think I'm getting a little nervous about how to tackle this."

"Don't be nervous. All you need to do is tell the truth about Chihopo and add your, um, flair. There's no one who can tell them," he paused, obviously calculating the whims and finer filaments of Mikalla's prickly soul, "the *truth* quite like you can."

Mikalla turned away from Zac and fought off an inauspicious smile. "You seem to have thought about this a lot, Zac. And the confidence you have in me is inspiring." Mikalla put his right hand to his chest. "I'm gonna have to dig down deep for this one—really drill into the ol' creative well and come up with a pail of truth that emboldens our people… and our kingdom," Mikalla said. He shook his fist on the last few words.

"His Holiness will be pleased to hear that."

"But in order to do this," Mikalla started, "I'm gonna need another day to really nail this plot down. I'm feeling a burst coming on." Mikalla clenched his jaw and marched past Zac back into the studio before he dismissed his crew for the day and strode back home. Zac stood by and watched as Mikalla zigged around him and went on. In a way, that was all Zac could do with Mikalla. That was all he was *sent* to do.

"Wait! Mikalla, quickly, before you go. Wait, please turn around. Yes, and I apologize for this, but what specifically—just so I can report it—will you be doing in your absence from the studio today?"

Putting you out of a job, and maybe out of having a head, thought Mikalla. The striped-and-gilded virtuoso turned around and, with focused, smug rage, stomped toward the bureaucrat. All his men were watching, waiting. Zac stood his ground, still stone-faced. Yet somehow, there was a wealth of expression in his lack of one—standing like a statue in the face of the animated artist. Facing each other in the middle of the courtyard, the two were a clash of color and canvas.

"Me?" Mikalla raised his eyebrows. "I'll be building a ladder to peer above the clouds and siphon the very light that gives the gods their power," he said, nodding. He stepped even closer to Zac. He softened his voice. "That's what I'm going to be doing. And when I do it, I won't be *absent*, I'll be everywhere."

"I'm going to put you down as 'writing.'"

"You will." *You'll put me down as whatever you want to. That's what your type does.*

Zac was satisfied enough, smug in his own quiet way. Mikalla walked out. The ears of his crew perked with every *clack* of his sandals.

This is not okay, he thought, safely removed from the studio's campus and away from the prying pupils of the mouse-like man.

You want writing, Zac? How 'bout you write this then: Your mother protected you beneath her bosom your whole life. That's why you suck the teat of the state to get by and buy your cheating wife some stupid, meaningless gold! What a skinny pig! What a disgrace to life and all things honorable!

Mikalla would show him and the rest of those nobles a story. And he hoped they liked the coarse feeling of wool over their eyes. *Blind, rapacious bastards.*

Chapter 6

T ozl had a slender, young face with high cheekbones, sparkling eyes, and a wet comb-over kept trim. Tozl's life was one big career fast-track he was happy to shake, nod, and smile through, so long as it sucked him closer to the vortex of power at the center of Idaza. He had sinewy arms that were often wrapped in fine silk robes. He liked closed-toed, black, leather sandals with hard soles that echoed with each step. What he invested in most were his shimmering white teeth—a rare sight in the kingdom, even among the nobility.

As the youngest diplomat in Idaza, Tozl was not quite weary of the long, lonely nights of travel many of his older colleagues— with families and shelves full of dusty accolades—were accustomed to. In fact, he found the open road and far-reaching scope of political diplomacy exhilarating. When he wasn't beaming and winking at foreign leaders, he was floating around the bustling bazaars of exotic city centers with a pocketful of government gold and an itch to spend it. His boundless ambition imbued him with a kind of swiftness he carried everywhere. His electric zeal made him a favorite during his schooling years and, eventually, in the Idaza Ministry of Foreign Affairs.

He always received orders and jobs from the Idaza Minister of Policy, though this time was different. For the Chihopo conference, he was briefed by Secretary Kitan on what to say and do, but he thought nothing of this irregularity. Actually, he thought very little in general. Tozl was an agent of the state without any real agency—a silk-clad servant smiling his way to the center of the vortex.

Tozl now found himself being sent to the Chihopo countryside for his next diplomatic appointment. Upon arrival, he was escorted to a spacious suite on a cliff overlooking the ocean. He had direct access to the majesty of the aqua sea and a clean room to lay his head but was perturbed by the gross lack of amenities he was otherwise accustomed to. He had to draw his drinking water from a nearby well, sat on plain furniture, and had no original art hanging anywhere.

"Odd," he said, brow furrowed, scanning the room.

His escorts—a short, thin man with a long chin and a burly woman with her hair tied—bowed in unison once Tozl entered the room. "Your caravan will be ready for you tomorrow, sir. His Majesty will meet with you at midmorning. Be ready for the ride at dawn. Welcome to the Kingdom of Chihopo."

As they turned to leave, Tozl eyed the long, sheathed daggers strapped at both their sides. Once the door closed behind them, he let out a caveman grunt and flung his silk robe onto the crooked table. He felt the red light of day escaping him through the window and made a break for the oceanside. His wallet clinked with each step on the way down the wooden stairs of the beach cliff, where he went in search of weak women and powerful potions that would satiate his empty spirit until dawn.

Chapter 7

I t was a bad dinner. Throughout the meal, Mikalla's body picked up on some distant aspect, somewhere between the smoky, gray lines of decency and deception. It was a quivering sense in his gut—while eating with his beloved wife—that told him something just wasn't quite right. It may have been her tone, aloof and hollow—*but that was normal*—or her slanted glance, but there was an element of Jani oozing a strange suspicion that tilted the artist's insides with a green unease.

The sky was painted red at dusk. A servant pulled out Mikalla's chair for him, seating him to face Jani in the dining room.

Mikalla always vied for a more ornate dining display, but Jani insisted on a large, round table built functionally for her policy meetings. As usual, she got her way. Although the Inner Gardens had a structure built specifically for policy advisers, Jani would see to it that she hosted the Idaza Department of Education at their house, where she could control the flow of servants and amenities at her will. She laid out the name tags of the committee members ahead of time and assured them it was so the chefs could know who ordered what. "Please make sure everyone sits where they were placed!" she would say with a grin.

While growing up, food, money, and clothes were never scarce in her house. However, as the youngest of six children, the things that fed Jani's soul—affection, attention, agency, and connection—were competed over constantly by the squabbling siblings. Meaningful staples of the human spirit such as these things were like carcass scraps to vultures in Jani's house. When she was eight years old, she remembered scampering through the halls toward the family courtyard. It was a rare time when their father was home without work to do or meetings to attend, and the little girl was overjoyed at the thought of sitting on her daddy's lap and getting a warm hug and kiss.

While she was running as fast as her tiny feet could carry her, an outstretched leg from behind one of the columns in the hall popped out right in front of her. Before her infantile brain could stop or think to evade it, she fell headfirst onto the stone floor, with only her wrist to break her fall at the last moment.

Before she could cry, before she could scream, she held her bent wrist up to her face. It was now red, misshapen, and twisted at a disturbing angle—broken. From behind the column where she was tripped, she saw one of her older brothers leap out and sprint toward the family courtyard where Jani was initially going. He gave one glance back at the eight-year-old girl sitting shocked, in a white dress now soaked in gravel and mud, before continuing to run toward their father.

Jani broke down. She hyperventilated, yelped, and sobbed like a runt pup whose mother had left her for dead. The stone floor was cold and hard, yet it was the only thing that seemed to numb her pain. Her house was too large for anyone to have heard the screams until much later, when a servant spotted her and immediately brought her to a medic.

Even after the incident, Jani didn't dare tell anyone the truth of what happened to her, for fear of far worse pain and torment from her siblings if she ratted. She learned the value of holding her tongue, and that proved to be a political virtue later in her life.

Although she went to the most noble schools with the best teachers in the kingdom, the most she ever learned was from her own family. It was in her own house that she got a taste for the cold, hard ground and, with it, a taste of the world unique to her. She learned to despise the smallest and the weakest, and most of all, herself. What she never realized, though, was that she and weakness were one and the same; status and security could not purify her heart, nor could it shield her from the intense self-hatred she'd learned from a childhood of emotional neglect.

Jani was underhanded when she could be, hard-nosed when she had to be. She was a true gilded aristocrat; King Oro was her first cousin, her father was a high priest, she was married to Mikalla, and she herself was the Minister of Education. Going against her in any sort of serious way also meant going against the kingdom itself, so she was seldom challenged by anyone.

Still, she held a toxic contempt for those who did not stand up to her—the same contempt she felt when she gazed at her own reflection.

"You're home early." Jani stared at Mikalla.

Mikalla poked at his food. "Yep, we made good strides today, but then I hit a creative block and sent everyone home. How was your day, though? Did your meetings go well?"

Jani finished chewing and took a sip of wine to wash the bite down. She cleared her throat, looked up at Mikalla, and gave a curt nod. "Good," she said with a half smile, looking away.

Mikalla continued poking at his food, still failing to take a bite. "Anything exciting happen…?" Mikalla trailed off, grasping for some distraction to ease his mind of its anxious grip. *Why does this seem competitive? I don't have space enough for this; I don't have the heart to grapple right now—to choose between covering or displaying everything that's not constant.*

"What do you mean?" she said in a hollow voice, still chewing.

"Well, did you make any progress? Any big decisions?"

Jani dropped her silver fork onto the ceramic plate. "Nothing too crazy." She leaned forward slightly. "What about yourself? Anything you want to share?"

"Well…" Mikalla started. Jani intently eyed her husband's facial expressions, hanging onto every cheek quiver, brow flick, and lip bite, no matter how subtle. She scrupulously recorded his face—no twitch went unaccounted for. "For the first time ever today, I was… I was actually *given* a story to tell." Jani watched as his whole body rocked to and fro, swaying like the long branch of a lone willow tree, lost to the whims of the wind. He touched his face.

"Given?" Jani sounded surprised. "Who's dictating *you* a story to tell?"

Mikalla swallowed without a bite of food ever reaching his mouth. "King Oro."

Jani hesitated a split second, blinked a few times, then widened her eyes as she looked back toward Mikalla. "*King Oro?* Wow. That sounds pretty important."

"Yep," Mikalla said, still staring at his food.

"What kingdom is it about?" Jani asked.

"Uhh, I never said anything about another kingdom."

Jani paused and picked her fork back up. She signaled to a servant standing in the doorway to fetch more water. "Yes, well, I just figured that maybe another kingdom would be involved, or something along those lines… So, is it about another kingdom? Or no?"

Mikalla looked down at his crowded plate. His stomach was doing flips, and now he felt his head doing the same. It gave him a full feeling to see Jani backpedal like that. He didn't know quite why it made him feel good, but the feeling quickly faded back to thick, green nausea. "I need to go lie down or something. I feel sick." He stared at Jani, head pounding, waiting for a nod or flick of flippant approval.

Jani, noticing this, tried to hold Mikalla awhile longer. "Everything okay, Miki?" she asked.

Mikalla was turning pale green now. "I'm fine," he said. "Is Coyote in his room?"

The servant placed a full cup in front of Jani on command. She took another big gulp. "He is, but he's sleeping. Anyway, it seems like you're very worked up, but remember that I'm here to *help*. I'll be there to watch and support you with whatever you need." Her voice softened. "I love you, Miki, and I'll always have your back."

"I know—trust me, I know. I love you, too. I think it's just a passing thing, but I really need to go lie down," Mikalla said.

Jani glanced at his full plate and let out a sigh. "Go ahead," she said. "Maybe we can talk later?"

He pushed his chair out and made a break for the stairs.

"Make sure you drink some water, Miki!"

Jani watched him scamper out of the room and heard his flitting footsteps ascend to the second floor. She gritted her teeth and, with a dismissive sweep of her arm, commanded the servants to clear the table. Jani's thoughts went in rapid circles, red from their fury. Immediately, she thought the worst: *He's up to something. He can't really be sick. And if he is, then why? That same weakness within him is rearing its fickle head.*

She grimaced. Thirty-eight years of life and five as the Conjurer, and yet he's still just a big child—he hasn't learned a thing.

Chapter 8

Not all soldiers wield spears. Not all soldiers march and stand at attention. Some soldiers, like Tozl, wear silk robes, have pearly white teeth, and engage in handshakes instead of bloodshed.

Tozl woke up to a cool, salty breeze and the early prospects of a sunny day filtering in through his window. He yawned. He saw a clay cup on its side on the floor next to his bed, its mystery contents congealed in a puddle on the ground. He took a sniff.

"Ughhh!" Salty sweat, heavy muscles, and tired, sore joints plagued him. He sat up with a raspy groan and raised his sinewy arms. His weary face resembled worn leather that had been soaking in alcohol—creased, folded, with bags under his bloodshot eyes. His silk robe lay where he'd flung it yesterday.

Boom! Boom! Boom!

The room shook like a mini earthquake. Tozl shot up and ran for the door. His face tingled, and his heart was a nervous bass drum. He stopped halfway to the door and turned back to grab his robe. His foot landed in the mystery puddle, and he furiously shook it off, hopping to the table where his robe lay.

Boom! Boom! Boom!

"I'm coming!" Tozl yelled, shimmying on the robe and corkscrewing his wet foot on the rug. He looked out the window and saw a caravan of three horses, all of them saddled, two of them occupied with riders. Both riders stared at the house.

Tozl crammed his feet into his sandals and opened the door to a tall mustachioed man with a balding head and a green tunic too small for his bulging frame. "Saddle up," he said gruffly, "you're late."

The horses clopped along the dirt roads of the Chihopo countryside. Tozl's ride was particularly skinny. "His backbone's poking me. Anything you guys can do?" he said. The escorts just laughed and carried on riding. The horses continued to kick up dust. If there was anything abundant in that countryside, it was dust. The sparse huts were covered in it, as were the people.

Tozl saw few travelers, and even for a rural countryside, it seemed desolate. They stayed on the road for what felt like hours. The only thing that seemed to have any vitality was the screaming sun on the horizon. In Idaza, the sun beamed and embraced the people. Here in the Chihopo countryside, it somehow seemed vengeful. It glared down and cast black puddles of shadow onto the dirt like tar poured on the earth.

After a morning of endless clopping, they stopped at a well. "How much longer?" Tozl asked in between hungry gulps.

"We're close," one of the escorts said.

Now hydrated, the cobwebs in Tozl's brain melted off, and he saw the silhouette of a city in the distance. He began going over his notes for the meeting. Secretary Kitan had emphasized that this was his "most vital assignment," and that he "couldn't miss a beat" with the king. Tozl hardened his resolve and felt a shot of adrenaline course through him—no lack of amenities would keep him from completing this mission and returning to Idaza with even more dignity and trust in the eyes of the royal court. He was determined to make it happen and advance through the ranks.

He visualized shaking Kitan's hand in the royal palace, looking into his welcoming eyes, and seeing a smirk of gratitude on his face after he'd so deftly navigated this act of diplomacy. He pictured himself standing in the center of the throne room and being applauded in front of King Oro. Tozl flashed his toothy grin, and the sullen horses clopped onward toward the silhouette of the steaming, dusty city. He was Tozl, the starry-eyed cynic, the perfect agent to the crown—with an empty mind and a racing heart.

Upon arrival at the Chihopo capital, the horses slowed to a walk. Tozl saw thin, bare markets and thin, bare people. Not everything in the city was brown, but a lot was. It resembled Idaza in a way, except every layer of its vibrance had been peeled off. There were no canals, and most of the buildings were nothing but dull shanties. Unlike Tozl's countryside dwelling back home, the city was inland toward the desert, and there was no breeze to cool his fried skin.

***

A royal attendant with a straight back, a straight mouth, and a straight ponytail pulled out a chair and seated Tozl at a table in the dim ballroom of the Chihopo royal palace. The gray room had unlit metal torches on the walls. The only light filtered in through the long, rectangular windows overlooking the brown city below.

After a few minutes, King Mirne entered the ballroom with two guards, who stayed by the doorway. He was old but not frail, hairy but not unkempt, pensive but not anxious. He had the look of someone who had the world on his shoulders but was used to the weight. He pulled out a chair for himself and sat down across from Tozl like a lion settling beside a sheep. There was only decisiveness in his voice.

"So, what do you think of the city, my boy?"

After Tozl got up from kneeling, he switched on his flagship smile. The king's gaze consumed him. "It's really charming, Your Highness. I was impressed with your people as well."

"Really? What about my people impressed you most?"

"They keep to themselves and shoot straight. Exactly how people ought to be. I know I could learn a thing or two from some of them," Tozl said.

"It would appear you already have, my son. You know, recognizing one's own faults is a mark of true wisdom."

"Well... yeah. I—I guess I meant that I *commend* it. It's not necessarily a fault of mine, per se."

King Mirne folded his hands, unmoved. "You said you could learn something from people who are straightforward. Therefore, you recognize it as a weakness in yourself."

"Well, honesty is certainly a virtue, and I think we could all do a li—"

"Are you sure you weren't impressed most by their rib cages, or their dusty huts, or their sickly horses?" Mirne cut him off. There was heat in his eyes.

"Sir, I—"

"You may call me 'Your Majesty' or 'Your Highness.' Either will do, thank you."

"Your Majesty—"

"I received the letter from Secretary Kitan last week. I agree to twenty percent of his embezzlement of the budget of Idaza's military campaign, and we'll even forfeit our riverbank territory in the south to make this work."

Tozl straightened up. "That's—that's wonderful! Now, what's the situation going to be for your troops? Total retreat?"

"Your legion is going to waltz into a few hundred rogues and barbarians burning some land and picking their own asses. They might kill a farmer or two, nothing serious. The conflict will be wrapped up by you guys without expending much of anything, at which point the people of Chihopo will graciously be endowed with a fifth of Idaza's military tax collections, many thanks to Mister Kitan."

Tozl sighed and stretched for a second. It was not customary to do so in front of royalty, but he felt oddly comfortable with Mirne now.

"So, surrender is sweet then?" Tozl asked. His smile returned.

"It is to save my people."

Tozl knelt and bowed. "Your Majesty, it has been an honor, and your people will get the help they need because of your generous compliance."

"Yes, indeed. I can sacrifice my pride so my people can return to their former glory. That is what a true king does. That is what a government does. It seems like Idaza may have forgotten about that idea, though: sacrifice. They left it behind with their greater kings of the past. Now, that drunkard just has childish half-men like you working for him."

The insult was a drop of poison that embedded in the sticky mass in the back of Tozl's mind, but he submissively half smiled through it. It was small, lethal digs like these that made Tozl's psyche a tangled minefield too painful for him to explore—and his surface of grandeur and status covered it all up in a polished veneer. "I commend you, Your Highness. You're a wise and gracious—"

"Commend yourself. We may not be decadent like the fairy folk in Idaza, but the people of Chihopo have a steel dignity that doesn't succumb to cunning, womanly games."

"Of course, Your Majesty."

King Mirne got up from his chair and stared down at Tozl. "Your secretary's a snake, boy, and the Idazan people are mice. You know what snakes are loyal to, son?" He paused for a second, flaring his nostrils. "Their stomachs."

The king relieved Tozl of his kneeling and shook his hand to signify the deal was done. Mirne reached the exit of the ballroom and turned around. "May Idaza enjoy their faux victory. I hope you're getting a piece from Secretary Kitan for this, too."

While Tozl waited for the escorts to file in, he stared out at the brown city through the arched windows. He watched people lugging buckets and baskets pass by, but they looked like ants from the palace window. It was true that Tozl seldom thought for himself. He poured his focus into his effectiveness at his job and how his masters viewed him—from the side, from the front, as a professional, and so on. His swiftness of action and lagging mind allowed him to advance quickly up the ranks of society.

While staring out the window of the ballroom, a sudden thought about Kitan whizzed through his idle mind. Then another one came. And another. Tozl was bombarded with a slew of thoughts all at once. Kitan's face swam through the toxic images of his brain—the words that oozed out above the secretary's angular, drooping jaw made him shiver all over.

Later, he was escorted back to his oceanside suite. He packed up and headed back to Idaza with a wealth of things to occupy his destitute mind.

Chapter 9

Mikalla cleaned his own vomit that night.

After rushing upstairs from the table, he spewed his guts on the ground before even reaching their toilet. He was too embarrassed to ask a servant to wipe it up and, for a reason he didn't understand, too nervous for Jani to find out. He was used to being nervous, but he'd never had anxiety overwhelm him to the point of vomiting—nausea that gripped his entire body and ravaged his insides.

By many who knew him well, Mikalla was referred to as a free spirit. By those who knew him best, he was referred to as independent. Despite the labels placed on him by the people he called his friends, he was fine with others dictating his life. Unlike many people, who—in his eyes—deluded themselves, he accepted it as a fact of life that, as soon as a person was born, they were shackled to much and commanded by many. Even he, steeped in a great noble status at the top of society, knew this to be the truth of life.

But this shackle imposed on his pure expression had gone too far for the Conjurer. This command, this hurdle, this idea of tricking the public to give up their own money and children for a war that, deep down, he was sure was unnecessary, while confining his craft inside a bureaucratic box: That just wouldn't do. In fact, Mikalla's guts had more reason than he did; his pink insides bore more wisdom than his mushy mind ever could. His bubbling body ached because it knew the artist's life was pointless without the freedom to create. It may have been selfish, it may have been insubordinate to the crown, but it was true. Mikalla was an individual who told stories about individuals, who carved the ornamented depths of an individual's soul in his works. And to have a purpose, to be willing to die for a cause—was that the highest form of living?

Corn and avocadoes satisfied his stomach. Gold lined his wallet. But those things just supported the body—yes, the body. The best things in life were non-sustentive, the things you couldn't eat, touch, or see that could strum the Promethean filament within. Mikalla understood this, and so he saw clearly the options presented to him with this conflict: He could either live cleanly in a sterile paradise or drown in the richest blood of birth and rebirth—painful, meaningful perpetuity. The choice was only Mikalla's to make, and he had to accept one of those fates by the time the ceremony began in less than a week.

Mikalla was well-situated in his golden prison, and every day, he clinked the bars with a smile and a song. But no longer could he continue to sit in the golden cell and live in his truth.

While cleaning the blotched tiles, he dropped a question on himself like an anvil: *Who am I?* He searched, he pried, he pained himself for an answer as he wiped up the green, chunky stomach bile puddled on the tiles of his bathroom floor. He had seldom ever ventured outside of the capital city, let alone the kingdom or the region, but he did explore *himself* often. And he looked for himself, desperately, all over those tiles.

He knew he was not his job title or, even less so, his public ethos. He wasn't anything public, for that matter. He wasn't who he was married to, though he cared for her, nor his kin, though he loved him with the whole of his heart, nor his ruler, though praise be to the king, nor the adoring audience that clapped for his work, though he reveled in their praise. He wasn't even his own words. Like water poured through a grate, he could be identified somewhere underneath and between the lines of his own dialogue.

He was himself when he got out of his own way. He was less of an archive and more of a breathing, bubbling blaze of the stories within himself. When those stories could not be released somehow, his vital flame atrophied and cooled.

Maybe his nervous vomit was just that, though; the green bile was a story within him that projected out of the churning depths of his gut rather than through a pen or a puppet or a drum. But even that fact he was unsure of, much like most of the other things in his life at that moment.

It was not powerlessness that made him so sick and anxious. Quite the contrary—he was given *too much* agency in a fallen world. He was in a mountainous predicament carved out of pure, dumb luck. In a kingdom where so many scrambled for influence over the direction of the law, the gold, and the warriors, he was given the key to the hearts and minds of everyone on an embroidered pillow.

After scrubbing a little longer, he saw the bathroom tiles restored and, with them, his appetite. But there was no time to eat. Somewhere in his tile-wiping musings, he saw a way forward, a story to tell. Mikalla was a basilisk running on water when he zipped up to his study to plot the story. At his desk by candlelight, the vital flame spilled out of him onto the page in the form of an experience for the people of Idaza. It would be a ceremony they would never forget.

Chapter 10

King Oro sat down at the meeting in plain white robes with a large jug of water by his side. His face was vexed. They were in a policy room outside of the palace, somewhere in the Inner Gardens, for a meeting King Oro had called. General Jax sat to his left, followed by Lukas, the Idaza Minister of Finance; Zac, whose formal title was Adviser to the Royal Court; Secretary Kitan; Coozma, the highest-ranking priest in Idaza, who replaced Jani's father shortly after he passed; and Jani.

"The flow of wine and splendor has ceased for me," King Oro said. "I have no time now for anything but the protection of what has been afforded to you as citizens of Idaza." He slapped the table with both hands. "My grandfather's father, Menizak the Great, united the tribes of the Mesoas Valley. It was still a village of straw and stone when my grandfather took control and made it a true empire. He opened up trade throughout the region, tightened the law, and expanded Idaza's borders. My father did the mining and the building and lifted Idaza to the wealthy hub we know it as today. Then, I realized something—if I sit idly by and lose even an inch of what my father bestowed unto me, I'm nothing but a skid mark on my family's great lineage and a violator of the divine trust the gods have given me. And I won't let that happen!" King Oro balled his hands into fists and smacked the table again with twice the force.

Clapping trickled in, then the room erupted in applause. Secretary Kitan stood up for an ovation, making faces and nodding his head fervently. The other five in the room quickly followed suit and stood. King Oro sat unaffected. He gulped his water and commanded everyone to sit down after some time.

"Now, in some way or another, you may know why I've called you in here today. But if not, I will waste no time in turning it over to Secretary Kitan, who will give the rundown on the Chihopo conflict," King Oro said.

Secretary Kitan was dressed in his usual long black robe. He leaned back to cross one leg over the other and placed an elbow on the table to reveal his arachnid hand. It contorted and jittered as he started, "Gracious people of the court, just the other day, it came to my attention that one of General Jax's scouts spotted military aggression to the north of our farmland, bordering on Chihopo. The diagrams on your pamphlets are indicative of the conflict as scouted, as well as where we think it could lead to a… *grim* scenario," Kitan said, taking his time with every word. "Now, I have sent a diplomat there to speak with King Mirne himself to vie for peace. 'Twill be a spear in the dark, but peace is *always* worth a shot…"

"Who'd you happen to send?" Jani asked.

"I sent Tozl, our *finest* risin—"

"He has no reverence for the gods!" Coozma interjected. "He's not a worthy vessel to send for a job so delicate."

Kitan was unfazed. "Coozma, you are a divine vehicle for holy wisdom, and you un*doubt*edly should have been factored into the decision of which diplomat to send. I can assure that you will be consulted next time. But for now, Tozl is young and charming, and his track record is pristine."

Coozma settled down. "Thank you, Secretary. It's just important that Chuxpapa and Tiotli have more agency in a situation like this. May they smile upon us anyway."

"Indeed," Kitan said.

"Jax, anything to add from a strategic point of view?" King Oro asked.

Jax raised his eyebrows and looked around the room. All eyes were fixed on him. "Um, yes. Ahem. This campaign will be based on the fury of our fighters and the speed at which we come at the enemy. That said, I think we need to invest in five hundred full archers, plus metalwork and equipment. And, um, speed will be an issue, too, so we'll need refurbished spiked soles for at least two legions."

Lukas, the finance minister, began fidgeting in his seat before Jax had finished. "Two whole legions? Five hundred fully equipped archers?" Lukas spoke like he was muttering to himself, but he projected his voice so the room could hear.

"Yes, sir," General Jax replied. He gave a curt nod in response to Lukas.

"I understand I'm no militarist here, but I know Chihopo. They have a downtrodden economy, and a pitiful drought is causing a resource shortage. Even if they're going to break the treaty and get desperate, knowing what *I* know, we could squash any raid they try with the resources we already have, never mind all of this," Lukas said.

Kitan jumped into the fray. "Mister Finance Minister, with all due respect, the importance of the fertile plains to our north *cannot* be understated. An inch lost there is a mile and a swath of people lost down here. We can't have that, now, can we?"

"We have a shell of a defense force there, even with our retreating campaign reinforcements from the east," General Jax said to support Kitan's point.

"Oh yeah, I forgot about the eastward campaign retreat. We have that there, too? I'm sorry, but there's no *way* we don't crush any resistance from Chihopo with that reinforcement on top of our boundary guard," Lukas said.

"Lukas, I understand your concern, but our main job here is defense and the protection of the empire. I know what we need to make this happen because I have the experience on the ground, having served Idaza for decades," General Jax said in his usual matter-of-fact tone.

"I don't know what to say here. We'd have to raise taxes and limit imports for this," Lukas said. His eyes skittered about, eventually landing on King Oro. "Your Majesty, as the Minister of Finance in charge of the monetary prosperity of your kingdom, I wholeheartedly advise against an expenditure like this. It would put us *gravely* in debt. Now, if we could look at scaling ba—"

"Your Majesty, I know what needs to be done. I've proven it time and time again, and I am saying we need this budget for the task at hand," Jax said firmly.

"For the protection of Idaza and all of its vast riches and culture. For *your legacy*," Kitan pressed, reinforcing Jax's point.

"Very well. I am hereby approving the proposal laid out by Jax. Lukas, you will be tasked with itemizing the campaign budget, and it will go to Secretary Kitan for final edits and approvals," King Oro said.

Lukas hid his disgust at the king's decision under a paper-thin veneer of soft-spoken objectivity. "How do we plan on selling this to the people?"

"Mikalla has a handle on that," King Oro said. "I briefed him yesterday on the task at hand."

"Zacatilanzec, what is the update with that?" Jani asked.

"It's… lagging some. He ended the meeting early yesterday and said he needed more time. I have the notes here." Zac slid amate parchment over to Jani's side of the table. "I'll be in the studio with them today for more updates. He seemed to be pretty inspired when he left."

Secretary Kitan intercepted the stack of parchment and looked it over. His head bobbed and brows furrowed as he flipped the papers one by one. "How did you get this? Are you overseeing the story?"

Jani spoke up on his behalf. "Zac is making sure the story is straight for the people with Mikalla, to make sure things go... smoothly." She nodded to herself like a trained seal. "I sent him."

The entire room fell silent.

Chapter 11

I n the studio that day, Zac sat in his usual empty seat as a lone member of the audience, inking the parchment as he observed the rehearsal like a scientist discovering a species. Mikalla lit a mock projection flame to show on the theater rock. He put his hand in front of it, showcasing shadows to the part of the crew responsible for the puppets. "They need pointy ears, like *this*," Mikalla said, bending his hand to form the shadow of a goblin-like head onto the slab of rock, "and we need a sea of them. We'll have to pan across hundreds."

Zac continued to ink the parchment. He scrawled the words, *"Chihopo citizens as goblins. Hordes of them to be shown. Dehumanize."* Although he was sent there to observe and annotate, he personally liked the way Mikalla seemed to be steering the production.

"Get their noses and claws, too. The features need to be *accentuated*," Mikalla said. "The features *are* the characters." The members who gathered around were nodding. "Nik, I need you to replicate the crowd prop with the adjustments necessary. Make one and show me before you make the rest." He gave more direction to the visual crew, making examples with his own hands and the loose objects in front of the projection flame. Mikalla then strode down the walkway between the empty audience chairs to the back of the studio.

Zac swiveled his chair around to face him. Mikalla walked in the middle of the instrumentalists, waving his hands over his head. "Stop, stop. I need to be *cut*. I need staccatos from you guys. I need to *bleed*." Mikalla bent his knees and back when emphasizing the point. He whisked his hands and moved with his voice. He was in the middle of the drummers now. His face grimaced and bounced and smiled and fell into awe.

He then floated over to the flute section of the crew. They stopped as he approached, straightening their torsos and tightening their glutes. Mikalla curved his right hand. "Up, up, up, up... and *crash*!" Mikalla leapt down to all fours and smacked the ground. "*Crash, crash, crash!* You're making a wave, guys, and a good wave isn't pedestrian—it's violent and powerful and fluid and dangerous!" He pointed to one of the flute players. "You. From the top," he said, wagging his finger.

Zac watched this from his chair, scrawling notes as he went. The words *"violent—cutting—bleeding"* populated his page.

Chapter 12

King Mirne sat on his metal throne in the middle of the cavernous hall. An infant girl in a frilly pink gown was on one of his legs, climbing on his chest and touching his face.

"I gotcher nose, I got it!" the king said, taunting his daughter as he shook his fist and put his thumb in between his fingers. The Queen of Chihopo was a gaunt woman in her forties who always had her chin in the air. She had stringy brown hair and wore a thin burgundy cardigan. She leaned on one of the throne's headposts, which looked like a cane in her hands. Even as she looked down at the sitting Mirne, her head was angled up.

"Okay, baby, you need to go play with your brother in the west wing now. Daddy needs some privacy," the queen said. The king gently set the girl on the floor after laying a kiss on her cheek through his peppered beard.

"Okay, Laila, go play now. Daddy loves you."

The girl scampered off, and the queen squared her body toward the king. She sighed as she turned to watch her daughter leave the hall. "Look, I know how badly we need this, but I just don't know if it's a good idea to forfeit our territory on the riverbank. We only need one good season, and it's back to a surplus," the queen said.

King Mirne buried his forehead in his hand. "And when will that season come, Meliska? And at what cost? Our people are suffering *now*, and an angel is giving us gold instead of rain. The decision is final, and it's what Chihopo needs. Now."

"Mmm, it's a dark angel that bestows us with this gift, Mirne," the queen muttered.

Just then, a worried-looking man walked in. He hurriedly paced ten steps into the hall and took a jerky knee, his fingers moving even after he bowed.

"Setilus, what bid you to enter here?" the king said, removing his hand from his forehead and inhaling.

"Your Majesty, your graciousness, it's our foreign ambassador to Idaza."

"What of him? Have we received word back from him yet?"

"That's the issue, Your Highness. We haven't. No one has. The last communication we received from him was two moons ago."

"Well, just check the stall room. I'm sure something got held up." The king was unconcerned.

"We did. We double-checked it. But that's not all. Levi's guards... they came back here—"

"To Chihopo?" The king scooted closer to the edge of the throne.

"Yes, Your Majesty, to Chihopo. They said he got lost in Idaza. They woke up one day, and he wasn't in his quarters. Nothing was out of place, though. They looked everywhere."

"By the gods," the king said. He stood up, and the queen took a step back from the throne. "Bring the ambassador's guards in here at once. I'm getting to the bottom of this."

Chapter 13

King Oro commanded his guards to stay in the hall. There was urgency in his voice, sweat on his brow, and tension in his bones. He continued to walk past the pillars and march through the courtyard by the pool. Oro then cut through the royal dining hall to get to the throne room. This room had gold-spiraled beams, each fifty feet tall, mosaics of battle scenes strung along the walls, and stained-glass windows filtering the sunlight through a dizzying kaleidoscopic lens. It was as disorienting as it was enchanting. At times, though, enchantment and confusion were one and the same. Behind Oro's purple-cushioned throne were two twin waterfalls cascading into smaller streams that encircled the king's chair like a moat.

King Oro strode through the room, not bothering to lift his white robe as he waded through the crystal water. He went right past his throne toward the waterfalls in the very back. Without the gold and rainbow reflections of the light on the walls of water, it just looked like any other naturally occurring waterfall, except tamer. King Oro approached it and held his breath, diving into the very place where the water crashed after falling off the top of the rocks some twenty feet overhead.

When he was submerged, the gentle roar of the waterfall sounded more like a muffled bath faucet. Oro looked up at where the stream met the pool of water. Everything was different in the deep blue and black. To Oro, it was dreamlike. The water had no expectations of him, nor anyone. When he fanned his arms to the side, the water heeded and propelled him. Water didn't ask him for anything. It didn't think for itself because it wasn't sentient, yet it held great wisdom. When water met a cliff, it fell. When water met itself, it didn't war, nor complain, nor feud, nor break apart—it simply flowed and continued downstream. Sometimes, in the rare moments when Oro was in the water, he felt he was a part of it. He could be one simple molecule, the whole body itself, or something in between—somewhere downstream in time, flowing and melding with the whole of the water. King Oro, deep down, realized he was part of the great current, and he was fine with being exactly that—a continuation of the stream.

He swam up and poked his head above the surface of the water. From inside the cavern he was now in, the backside of the waterfall looked more like a smooth wall of flowing force, distorted by the many colors of the throne room. Oro climbed the stepladder from the pool of water and found himself in a black catacomb. He squinted through the darkness and flinched as he felt a tiny creature scurry past his feet. *God, I could go for a drink.* There were torches on the walls, and the farther he walked down the lone path, the more necessary they became. The echoes of his soaked steps were accompanied by the sounds of skittering and the squealing of claws, legs, and fangs in the blackness of the cave. It was impossible to identify the slight creatures lurking just out of sight. Oro could only catch flashes of spindly legs and black zipping by in the wobbly puddles of torchlight.

As he walked, Oro couldn't help but wonder how the conflict had come to this. *I'm at the reigns of a beast I can't control—it's bigger than me. If I hurt one person, another suffers—one on the other side. And what has being the king gotten me?* When Oro considered what he'd gained from his crown, only three things came to mind: dilemmas, treachery, and drink. And now he found himself in a cave, where work better left unseen resided. *And why? What did they do to deserve this?*

After a few more squelching steps through cragged rock, dots of feces, and mystery carcasses, Oro came upon a wooden wall. Apart from some small claw marks, it was clean compared to the rest of the dingy cave. It had a giant "M" carved in its upper center. He walked up to it and knocked three times.

"Tahautl Xichopotlit," King Oro said. His tone was guttural and assumptive, like he was swearing after losing a card game. Then, he stood still and paused there, silent. Oro's voice carried through the arches of the cave, bouncing around for a whole minute. The uproar was loud enough to startle the creatures within, and soon the whole cave fell into an eerie, black silence.

On the other side of the wall, Oro heard a clank of metal. Then another. Soon, there was a succession of them, *clank, clank, clank, clank*. The wooden wall rose from the ground and disappeared into a slit in the ceiling above. A chamber appeared in front of Oro, clean and lit with torches illuminating a large steel cage sitting in the middle. King Oro was welcomed by a mountain of a man near the entryway. He wore a black leather strap across his chest and matching headgear, so only his eyes showed. *And a man like this is at my disposal, ready to kill on a whim. And for what?*

"He's right here, Your Majesty."

King Oro stepped closer to the iron box. Cowering in it was a withered man. All he wore was a tattered burlap sack and a pained expression that fell somewhere between resignation and hatred. He had a scraggly beard, dirt-caked feet, and faint blue eyes. He looked like a failed oracle, a wise vagabond who may have been something in a past life.

"Ambassador Levi, *tsk tsk*," King Oro said, stepping within an inch of the iron bars. "Ya know, it's a shame things have gotten so… cagey." The king put his hands over his gut and guffawed at his own quip. Oro exuded a detached confidence and continued to peer at the guard. *Please just make this easy. It doesn't have to be hard. This can be the first step toward getting to the bottom of this.*

"I did nothing wrong," Ambassador Levi said. His voice came out drawn, scratchy, and tired for a body no more than forty years old.

"*You* may not have," Oro said, "but your pitiful, bearded, bastard of a king did. Oh yeah, he did a lot, like send troops to *my* farmland. Trying to take *my* territory."

"He wouldn't do that. He *didn't* do that! Who told you that?"

King Oro completely ignored his contention. *Why would he wonder where I got my tip? Why would that matter? Does he think my court is so plagued that I would be fed lies?* He gritted his yellow teeth and stuck his head almost inside the cage, piercing Levi's eyes with his. His round head flickered in and out of shadow. "Listen here, Ambassador. I'm going to give you one chance, and one chance only," King Oro growled. "Tell me, what are Chihopo's military ambitions, and what is your next move?" *I'm begging you, you pathetic little annoyance.*

"Your Majesty, please, please, our people are starving! There's been a drought, and we just need help. We wouldn't do this!" Levi said. His eyes cried dust, and he hacked up a throaty cough. Levi was an orphan in a way—abandoned by his kingdom and his guards, now on the precipice of certain, painful annihilation. All he could do was rock and sob and plead and tell the sharp truth that, no matter what, would turn around to cut him fatally. He went on, "Please, sir, I have no idea—I have nothing! I have children and a sick mother who need me." The ambassador bowed so low his forehead nudged the ground. "I'll do anything. I swear to the gods, I don't know. Please…"

The king turned back to the muscly, leather-bound man. "He's pretty convincing, huh?" Oro said. The man chuckled. "Heat him up. See if that gets him talking. Be ready to extinguish it once he does." The flicker of torchlight across Oro's face evolved into a wildfire as he spoke.

This has to work. This also can't be a bluff. But the pain in his eyes... What if he's telling the truth? The king hesitated. *What am I then?* How weak was his legacy if he couldn't discern between fake and real, if his enemies were really friends? The rancid cave, with its pressing darkness, was as muddled as his mind.

On the king's signal, the masked man grabbed a torch off the wall then lit a pyre on top of the cage where Levi was sobbing.

"Oh no... No, no, no, no, *no*! Please, please, I swear I know nothing!" Ambassador Levi screeched. "Nothing! Our people need food! *Ahhh*—" His words devolved into incomprehensible howling. He hopped around the cage, first on one foot, then the other. He jumped on his hands to relieve his feet from the hot metal. Oro and the guard started to hear steaming and sizzling. The ambassador got off his feet and laid on the parts of his body that were not yet cooked, but they soon burned, too. Within a few echoing minutes, Ambassador Levi became a writhing red nugget—a pulsating ball of flesh that could do nothing but spew and hiss and wail. He lay in a soup of his own blood and tissue.

The leather-bound man snickered at the anguish. The more Levi moaned, the more he mocked and chuckled. He started to throw rocks and gravel at Levi, laughing all the time, as if the ambassador's pain was fuel for a twisted, primal fire somewhere within him.

The dank room filled with the mist of simmering flesh and blood. The king's face went green, and he turned away from the scene. Oro felt like clawing his eyes out and scampering away from it all. *All that pain and no answer. All that...* The face of Levi flashed across his vision, first searing red then devolving into bubbling flesh. *Kids... did he have a son of his own... just like my father had? Did he... treat them well? The rocks. God, that's a bad smell... but the rocks—look at the way their dampness gleams like gemstones under the light of the flame. They move when they flicker… I bet the rocks can't feel any pain when my feet oppress the tops of their surfaces. So unlike humans.*

"Enough, enough!" King Oro shouted at the leather-bound man. Still shielding his face, he commanded the man to finish the job before he bolted out of the chamber with one hand over his eyes and one over his ear to block out the echoing anguish. Oro was halfway to the waterfall when he heard a distant thud. After that, all the noise left was the squelch of his steps and the skittering of claws and legs on the damp, rocky floor beneath.

Very few times in his life had Oro ever had to use torture as a device. But every time before Levi, he'd known it was the right decision. Each instance he'd executed torture before this, it had been an easy decision—a straightforward one. It was pain invoked against a villain, an enemy of the state. Now, with the mix of conflicts and interests and apprehensions he buried deep, he didn't know who the enemy really was. He'd gotten his information from Kitan, who was supported by Jax. But he hadn't gotten actual proof from anywhere yet. All he could do was rely on his trusted advisers. *But now I have a dead father on my hands, a dead servant to another father, a son of a mother. Maybe I'm the enemy.*

Chapter 14

K itan sent a handful of guards in black feathers, black linens, and black-striped faces to receive Tozl once he arrived at the outskirts of Idaza. They formed a brigade around him, said nothing, and escorted him through the city commons. Tozl looked around at the people between the shoulders of the guards. He felt the familiar hum of Idaza in stark contrast to the doldrums of dusty Chihopo. He stayed directly in the middle of the brigade, watching the flow of people everywhere, all around him. The markets were packed, and the alleyways were flush with stray cats and the collections of scraps they guarded from pesky children and hungry vagabonds.

Amidst the liveliness of the city, Tozl realized how helpless they all were. He was in the thick of the commons now, walking among the people, but still, he looked down on the whole of the city. He did not see the children, nor the parents, nor the merchants, nor the swimmers in the city. Instead, he registered the bustling commoners as ants scurrying on the ground.

Tozl saw all of this while he was led to the hungry snake's domain. He had no choice but to face the snake. He was caught in the middle of a desperate, dangerous game and didn't yet know how this snake would view him—was he an ant or an ally? In a world of snakes, ants, and more, he had no idea what he was—but he was about to find out.

The royal palace stood out at the center of the Inner Gardens. Every noble house clamored for the chance to live near the luster of the palace. A noble's value, as well as their family's, seemed to be determined by how close their house was to the king.

Kitan's abode was not like the other nobles', though. He lived on the edge of the Inner Gardens, tucked away where the commoners could not bother him and the nobles could not see him. The Inner Gardens were full of manors with tall glass windows and hanging chandeliers. Kitan had more of a bunker than a house, carved into the steep side of a secluded hill. It had few windows and fewer doors. Not many people had ever been welcomed into it.

The brigade trudged up the hill through a tangled forest. There were no set trails to Kitan's house, yet the black-clad guards seemed to be able to navigate fine without a path. Tozl had no idea this part of the Inner Gardens existed. He'd never seen so many trees at once in Idaza's arid climate, nor anywhere throughout his travels, for that matter. He was used to plains and dunes, and now found himself wrapped in an environment that felt alive, *sentient*. The canopy of trees was a cool tent enveloping the party in one big shadow. When the wind swept, the forest swayed, and millions of leaves sang a hissing opera.

Tozl heard creaks, groans, and chirps that all bled into white noise. It was like wearing earmuffs and dark, cracked sunglasses while traversing a terrain that shifted constantly—roots, rocks, and all. The shifting forest was intoxicating in the shadows as he wove through the crunching brambles. Tozl was relieved when they reached a high point in the woods and the guards pointed down to Kitan's shielded bunker. As if seeing clearly through the canopy shadows wasn't difficult enough, the home was tucked under branches and vines. The only way to discern it from the forest was the light coming through a metal-barred window in the side of the slope.

Tozl was escorted from the forest and ducked through vines and brush to enter the cave-like abode. Upon entering, he didn't look around but, rather, trained his view squarely on the back of the guard's head until he was led into the room, passing through no other doorways on the way there.

"How's my favorite diplomat?" Kitan said. The secretary sat at the end of a table, facing the only entryway to the confined box that was the room. He raised his gaze up to Tozl without moving his head. His arms rested on the sturdy, rectangular, wooden table, clasping a clay mug. Everything in Kitan's house was pristine, and each object conducted itself in the same manner. The mugs and chairs and even the ornaments were self-serious, every item serving a purpose.

Tozl never addressed his masters in anything but his best apparel—that is, until now. The dusty road of the Chihopo countryside had left his silk linens dirty and tattered. Kitan didn't seem to mind, though.

Tozl bowed so his head stuck lower than his waist. "I'm doing well. Can you tell I've done some dirty work?" He laughed, holding up his robe to show off the scuffs and dirt.

Kitan was not amused. "Dirty work? Is there something dirty about fulfilling your duty?" The air in the room turned frosty and gray.

Tozl laughed, playing off the remark as a quasi-joke. The guards remained at the single doorway behind Tozl, unfazed and unmoved.

Kitan's voice softened. "So, how did it go?"

"It went perfectly. He agreed to all terms and said they'd take a fifth of the proceeds, *and* we can take a swath of the riverbank territory," Tozl said. He walked a few parchment notes over to Secretary Kitan. The guards stiffened. Kitan began eagerly scanning the notes, and while his nose was still buried in the paper, he motioned for Tozl to take a seat.

"Would you care for a drink, Tozl? You know, I have wine imported from the south that came in just last week."

"That'd be fantastic, Mister Secretary. And some water, too, please," Tozl said.

The secretary motioned to one of the guards to fetch refreshments. "Please, just call me Kitan," he said. "I'm assuming Mirne hit you with all of that 'son' nonsense... trying to subordinate you."

"Ah, yeah, well, I'm assuming he was just doing his job, ya know?" Tozl had a deep, subconscious reverence for authority that showed itself even if it seemed that authority might not have jurisdiction over him. However, in one way or another, it always did.

Kitan ignored Tozl's comment. "Do you know why he does that, Tozl? Do you know why he calls you, a well-respected diplomat, 'son?' Do you know why he sits while you stand and stands while you kneel and leans back when you bow?" Kitan's voice sped up, and he raised his head to meet Tozl's eyes.

"I'm not sure. Why?" Tozl said.

"Because he has to. People like Mirne play with small gestures, not... sweeping *strikes*." Kitan looked up at the ceiling and drew an audible breath. Kitan's ceilings had the same disposition as the rest of the objects in his house: strictly functional. They were tools in a box, one part of a greater sum. They were high enough to suit any height and low enough to discourage anything other than walking or sitting.

Kitan looked back down at Tozl. He scanned the parchment notes again, checking for the finer aspects of the deal, then gazed back at the ceiling before flicking his eyes to Tozl once more. "Do you know why I sent you, Tozl?"

"Well, I think we have a good relationship at this point, and I was, uh, definitely up for the job. As always, of course."

"Exactly. You were the right person for the job, Tozl. But also, without a doubt, you are ascending quickly within the ranks." Kitan softened his mealy gaze and cracked a rigid, closed-lipped smile. "Soon enough, you'll be Minister of Foreign Affairs. And I don't want anyone to get in your way." Kitan sharpened his eye contact with Tozl. "Do you understand what I'm saying?"

"I do, sir."

"Are you sure, Tozl?"

"Yes, sir."

He views me as an ant, Tozl thought.

Chapter 15

L ate that night, King Oro lay above the covers and stared at the ceiling. It was completely silent in the palace, but he kept his ears covered. He could still hear the throaty anguish of Levi. He wanted to wake up and redo the day, walk into the cage and plead with the ambassador to tell him the truth. He wanted to tell the ambassador he was doing this for his people, and he needed an answer. He wanted to get the answer out of Levi, then hug him and let him know his family—his sick mother, his kids, his wife, whoever else was dear to him—was safe because he cooperated. He wanted to cry and look into Levi's blue eyes and thank him for all of the lives he'd saved while freeing him.

Despite the godlike agency the king had on a daily basis, all he could do now was sob in his bed. After the fact, all he had were his own tears, as if they alone would cool the immolated skin of the ambassador, after he'd ordered his body to be fried on a hot plate to a slow death. Oro tried to slow his breathing and calm down, but he couldn't keep from hyperventilating.

Oro shuddered out of his position, wiped his tears, and made himself as presentable as a lonely, traumatized man could look in the dead of night with no sleep. He burst out of his chambers in his open robe, shoving the guards outside his doorway.

"Is everything okay, Your Highness?" one guard said. Oro ignored him and continued down the hall with determination. The guards tried to pursue him.

As soon as Oro heard their steps, he stopped abruptly in his tracks. "Stay your ass right there," he warned.

The guards froze. And just like that, he disappeared into the black of the pillared hall, trekking down to the small, candlelit room where, not more than a few days ago, he and Mikalla had spoken together. The walled basement was still replete with barrels, bottles, and a resolute slab of oak laid on top of a tall wine barrel.

Oro threw himself onto the nearest stool and popped a cork to let the warm caress of the deep, sweet burgundy elixir melt away the restlessness of his insides. His neck began to relax, and his breath slowed to a manageable pace. The agonized screeches of Ambassador Levi faded, along with the edges of his vision. The candles' flames became scintillating stars floating across the wood grain sky. The teary streams from his eyes dried as he slipped slowly, fluidly, into the rippling burgundy dream state.

He thought back to his father. They shared the same protruding brow and not much else, in body or mind. King Menizak III was resolute and muscular; he looked like a warrior. He was seldom inside the palace—he was seldom in Idaza at all. His heart belonged on the frontier of the kingdom, where the mines operated and the many disjointed tribes sprawled about. As a younger man, Oro rarely saw combat, let alone the kingdom's border frontier. His older brother, Menizak IV, was constantly on the campaign trail with the king. Menizak IV saw battle, the front lines, and the raw struggle at the bloody core of humanity. He held his spear with ferocity, charged armies, and wore his kingdom's headdress like a leader should. Oro could still picture his father grasping his brother's shoulder, smiling into his eyes, and patting him on the back. Besides fighting together, Oro's father would joke with his brother, would eat with him, would read with him—loved him.

Oro remembered the day his father's heart turned to ice. He pictured it through a crystal lens. He heard the palace gates swing open from the courtyard, turned, and saw the king carrying his first son. Blood flowed from Menizak IV's chest as tears streamed from the king's eyes in rivulets. Shamans, medics, and priests scrambled in behind the king. But no number of bandages, herbs, or prayers could stop the blood. It was like using a twig for a scalpel's job; it was an impossible feat to keep Menizak IV alive. The king spent the night where he began that day: on the ground by his son, drenched in his blood, and soaked with his own exhausted tears. The only thing certain in his mind was despair—then and forever.

Oro saw the exact moment his father gave up. He watched his father's face, after so much sadness and fluid and bereavement, turn to stone. After that, for the king, there was no more sorrow. There wasn't much of anything for the rest of his life. His face stayed pale, his lips in a thin line. He let his beard grow and his muscles soften. From the day his firstborn son died a hero, he stayed in Idaza's interior, focusing on economic means and the improvement of city life.

After becoming the next rightful heir, Oro learned to govern as a homebody, and his lessons came from his father's newfound sedentary style—if, of course, it could be called a style at all. Oro's father strayed from his rampant militarism not out of choice, but because the spirit of Menizak the Great had left his body through his tears and his son's blood.

He thought back to some of his father's teachings before he passed: *"Your privacy is your weapon, Oro. Your distance from your closest adviser is your best guard. Always keep your distance."*

In Oro's eyes, the people of Idaza only became healthier and wealthier with every passing year, but his father just called them *decadent*. The king was too tired and detached to insult Oro. He was too forlorn to lash out, so he went about treating Oro like he treated everyone else—coldly, like an ox on a yoke that just had to plow and be done for the day.

When Oro made his rare trips outside the confines of the palace and its sprawling royal gardens, he stopped every time at the statue in the Inner Gardens. He would stand and look and hypnotize himself in Menizak's stone gaze. Every time, he would recycle the same thoughts, the same doubts as to whether that was really *his* ancestor. To Oro, he seemed less like a forefather and more like what the rest of the kingdom saw him as—an idea, an ancient, a *statue*.

And so he often saw his father's gaze when he blinked or dreamt. It was much like Menizak's stone glare. He felt the disappointment of all the past generations weigh on his shoulders. He saw no right way to turn, no good move to make, suffocating under the strength of high hopes and constant underachievement. He scorned his brother—the true, rightful heir—for dying. Much like the wounds in Menizak's chest, there was no high priest, shaman, or medic to heal the toxic roots of inadequacy buried deep within Oro's gut. Warring or not warring, building or not building, Oro knew he was a pointless pawn in his own lineage. That feeling, that burden, could only be lessened with a drink. But with each burgundy sip, it became harder to tame.

That pain, that anger, that shame—he wished every day for it to leave, but relief never came.

Chapter 16

The next morning, Oro sat on his throne like fungi sitting atop the moss of a tree. He smuggled sandbags under his eyes, and his arms hung limp. He kept a loyal drink of water by his side with a crusty piece of bread in his lap. The rush of the throne room waterfalls usually soothed him in the morning. Today, though, they were a cacophony that tore at his headspace with every drop.

Then, Oro heard footsteps. They were loud but not intrusive, steady but not rhythmic. It was Kitan.

"Your Stateliness," Kitan said with a bow. He entered the throne room with his hands behind his back and his head tilted up so his tapered, jutting chin pointed outward. The secretary knew that the more grandiose title he bestowed upon Oro, the more reaction he could squeeze from him.

"Well?" Oro said. His round, fleshy head rested on his bear paw of a hand like a toddler in timeout.

Kitan sighed. "King Mirne did not budge. He is maintaining his fix on the border and continuing his barbaric aggressions. I'm sorry, Your Majesty."

"So… no deal, then?"

"It would appear so, Your Kingliness. I hate to be the bearer of rotten news."

King Oro's jaw quaked. His fists became rocks. He stayed seated, but his brows rose. "Get Mikalla and Jax in the palace courtyard this afternoon. We have work to do."

Kitan knelt at the command. "As you wish, Your Highness." Then Kitan, looking away from the king, stretched his face into a long, wide smirk.

***

Mikalla and General Jax knelt before the king, and Secretary Kitan stood by his side. Oro looked down at the pair.

There was a stillness in the dry air that felt icy despite the warmth of the sun. It brought the courtyard to a kind of stasis that felt like a goose-down comforter layered the scene. It was as if every movement had to be deliberate. There were four chairs set up by the poolside under the shade of two nearby palm trees. Three of them were identically wooden, while the last one was cushioned with a tall headplate carved with the crest of the royal family. Each person sat coiled and still, with both arms flat on the armrests.

"Gentlemen, we have a Chihopo problem," King Oro said. "As you know, they're attacking our farmland to the north, and I've been informed that our last-ditch diplomatic efforts failed." Oro lowered his tone to a mutter. "Mirne still has a stick in his ass." His voice was strained, scratched, and froggy, like rusted chains dragged over gravel. King Oro took a deep, strenuous breath and continued, "Mikalla, how is the progress on the set?"

Mikalla eased back in the chair and let his strong cheeks animate a smile while his eyebrows danced along to the beat of his words. He didn't have to reveal the whole picture, only the snippets that got head nods and assurance from his easy audience. "It's going great. Basically, I figured that making the people of Chihopo human would be too relatable. So, what I'm doing is making them monsters. Ghoulish creatures, in fact. My goal is to make those Chihopo goblins small and pathetic."

Little did they know, Mikalla was telling the truth—but not the whole of it. He never mentioned how he planned on depicting Oro, nor the rest of the crooked Idazan government. He didn't tell them that in his story, Chihopo housed the victims. They were the sympathetic heroes who defended themselves from the rich and powerful Idazans. It was bloody, it was treason, it was the *truth*.

Nevertheless, Mikalla's hands flowed along with the easy music in his face, accentuating his points and acting as the vessels for his excitement. It wasn't feigned. It wasn't an act. Mikalla was purely authentic and candid in that moment, just as he always had been—just as he always *had* to be. To calculate the internal value judgments in Mikalla's head would be like trying to unravel a ball of yarn made of balls of yarn. How he felt about a given thing depended on innumerable heaps of variables he constantly managed in his heart at any given moment.

He led with his heart because he had to, because that was simply who he was. There was nothing inherently wrong or right about it. He was who he was because he was born that way, and there were no courses of action nor external circumstances that could have molded him differently. Deep within the opaque plunges of any soul is an innate nature tempered by the fiery heat of existence. To deny one's own nature, Mikalla thought, was treachery of the highest order. To him, denying oneself was a toxin greater than any one social ill that poisoned—it was treason of the soul.

In order for Mikalla to go along with an order, even from the king himself, that order would have to go along with his personal value judgments. And Mikalla, through the wizardry of narrative subtlety he knew better than anyone in the kingdom, made it so his morals could align with the king's commands.

King Oro looked down at his feet. "Good."

Secretary Kitan jumped in. *If Oro won't prod him, then I will.* "It has to be about fear," he said. "They are threatening our way of life, our very life source. Get to the heart of the conflict, Mikalla. Conjure up our identity and show them what Idaza really *is*. They should be begging to give up their purses after your ceremony."

Mikalla nodded emphatically and maintained laser eye contact with Kitan. Their heads nodded, their mouths quivered and danced, and their brows played along, but their eyes stayed locked in a frigid stalemate. Neither Kitan nor Mikalla looked away from each other. It was a meeting between rationale and impulse, both of them embodying the deepest reaches of human desire.

"Abso*lute*ly," Mikalla said. "Vulnerability can work wonders, and what's more vulnerable than a child?" Mikalla continued to nod slowly, timed with the fluctuations in his voice. He knew he was being used as a tool. What he was unsure of was who he was being used by.

Kitan looked over at the king, who still had his gaze fixed on the grass at his feet. *Is he even listening?* "Your Majesty? Anything to add? Maybe important details you'd like to throw in, or…?"

"Nope." The king sighed. He wanted to hide it. He wanted desperately for that sigh not to have been audible, to have been erased from existence, unheard by anyone in the courtyard. He wanted to be able to cope with the weight of his kingdom without apathy. He wanted to be able to internally justify the tears and blood of Chihopo without tearing himself apart. He didn't want to be entrenched in the raw, wrenching geopolitics of his time, didn't want to choose who lived and who died.

But he had to.

The effects on his body from the weight of the world could be seen in the bags under his eyes, the wrinkles on his forehead, and the dry rot of his wine-stained teeth. "I think that sounds good, Mikalla. Looking forward to the show."

Kitan jumped in with force and fervor, not taking his eyes off Mikalla. *Fine, I'll do it myself*, he fumed. "Mikalla, you need to at least give us the plot of the story in regard to the central conflict. We need to know things like how it starts, who the main characters are, and how the governments are depicted. What about the king? How will it end—?"

Just then, a man appeared on the other side of the courtyard. The stiff attention of the four refocused harshly on the newcomer. He wasn't dressed like a guard, nor did he exude nobility. To say the man was underwhelming in stature would have been a gross understatement. His shrill voice suited his diminutive frame. He was middle-aged but had little facial definition and long, unkempt hair, much like what would be expected from an adolescent boy in Idaza. As was customary, he knelt before the king as he approached the noble foursome. "Your Majes—"

"Yes, what is it?"

"Your Highness, Chihopo h-has sent a representative."

King Oro stood up from his chair. Kitan looked over his shoulder at the small man with pure, childlike curiosity. Mikalla was helpless and unequipped for this, still pondering Kitan's onslaught of questioning. General Jax just wore a leathery scowl aimed at the untimely visitor. For Mikalla, the interruption cleared the obscure, foggy atmosphere in the courtyard and heated the icy air to a boil. It gave him time to think about Kitan, his story, and his approach. When he glanced at Kitan, he saw an adversary.

"Bring him in," King Oro said through gritted teeth.

The man ducked out of the courtyard and began signaling frantically toward a part of the hall Mikalla couldn't see from his vantage point. Two stony-faced guards gripping feathered spears with white knuckles emerged with a middle-aged man between them. The man had lightly graying hair and a handsome face with the shadow of a beard. He was calm for someone who was shackled and bruised.

He bowed and greeted the king with certain dignity.

"My name is Daniel," he said. "I was sent here by King Mirne to retrieve Ambassador Levi." Daniel swallowed. "I carry no weapons, have come with no escorts, and bring no harm to the great Kingdom of Idaza." He looked directly at King Oro when he said this. He had shackles on his wrists, but not a trace of contempt could be found on his face.

The indignant king, still standing, took a step toward the messenger. With his meaty fists tightened and his nostrils flared, Oro spat at Daniel. "You listen here. Levi could have left any time he wanted to."

Daniel widened his eyes. For a brief moment, he expressed a kind of hurt astonishment, but then it passed as quickly as a tropical storm. "He *could* have? I—I didn't realize that… but Your Majesty, I just want to know where he is so we can return our beloved ambassador back to the Kingdom of Chihopo."

Oro winced. His skin began to burn and itch as he replayed the memory of Levi writhing, red and seared. While the man was pleading for his life in that cage, Oro knew instinctively Levi hadn't lied about his sick mother, nor about his family who loved him. Oro knew and understood it was he and he alone who had deprived that family of their caretaker. It was not a foregone conclusion that Ambassador Levi had to die. It was a choice, and a choice Oro made of his own accord. He made that man's skin fry, then took his life away with a word and a wave. The health of his kingdom was the health of many people, and Oro yearned to save lives without the death of many. He had seen death before, swaths of it, and all its destructive force. But his hands were tied, and his mind was in knots.

"Yet you come to me as a war criminal in my kingdom," Oro said.

"Your Majesty," Daniel's voice was soft, "I was sent in peace, and I came only to request this one thing." His head was fixed on Oro's feet, like a sheepish child being reprimanded.

At the words of Daniel and the thick pause in the air, General Jax's hard, empty, gray eyes turned fiery. His fists gripped the chair tighter, and the vein in his forehead became more pronounced. He shot up out of his chair, and in that instant, the attention of the courtyard gravitated toward him. "Kill him," Jax growled. He bared his teeth, eyeing Daniel like a lion would a wounded gazelle. "Kill him now."

At Jax's command, Oro's vision became sharp. His breath ticked up, and he swiveled his head, panning rapidly between Daniel, the guards with spears, and General Jax. Oro watched in slow motion as both guards raised their trusty tools of violence in unison above Daniel's head. The silver spear tips seemed to grow fangs and noses that smelled blood and craved it, too. The spear tips awaiting Daniel's flesh were the finest, most delicate precipices between life and death.

Oro had seen death. And here and now, he thought choosing death was the easy way out. As a king in conflict, succumbing to the deadly edges the sharp spears offered was weak. Oro, panicking and trapped in his own head, decided to choose strength over weakness.

"Halt! Don't do it!" Oro ran toward the guards with his bear paw hands waving like leaves in a gust of wind. At once, they stopped their plunging motion and put their weapons at ease by their sides. Daniel, who had his head down like a helpless lamb, turned his eyes up to behold the screaming monarch. He looked confused, renewed, and thankful. All Daniel was in the balance of things was a handcuffed pawn in a game full of kings and queens. As long as he was alive, though, that would have to do.

The courtyard became silent and still. The only sound was Oro's panting, and the only movement was his heaving chest. Jax had a dumbfounded look on his face as his mouth gaped open and his neck tilted forward. The general sat back down as if he'd never risen in the first place. He dared not speak. The servants, the guards, Mikalla, Jax, Kitan, and Daniel were all bound in an anticipatory prison—all at the mercy of the crown. At that moment, in the open air on the grass, surrounded by regal, pillared halls on all sides, all they could do was revolve around the emotional whims of their king.

It was perhaps because of Oro's usually complacent nature that his assertive moments were so effective. Often in his life, he sat back, drank wine, and relaxed on the heap of wealth his forefathers had wrought. Maybe it was only this lazy perception of Oro that made moments where he stood up and took control so powerful. Regardless of how and why they had all gotten there, neither the schemer, nor the artist, nor the general, nor the weaponed men, nor the foreigner had any say here. It was the king they waited on.

Jax may have commanded the military, but Oro commanded him. To forget or subvert that hierarchy would be to subvert the kingdom itself, and Jax—even with his dim wit and impulsive nature—still knew better than to do that.

Oro drew one big audible breath and slowed down his frantic hands and chest. His feet kicked into the grass, and his calves flexed. He stomped toward Jax, who was still seated in disbelief. The flame in the general's eyes had suffocated to sizzling ash.

Oro towered over Jax. "Never," he said, steam coming out of his nose, "do that again."

The king stood there for what seemed like the afternoon, piercing Jax with his eyes. After some time, the general fell on both knees with his head and chest to the ground. With a mouth full of the courtyard's grass, Jax paid his homage to the king. "Yes, Your Highness. It won't happen again."

With that, Oro's voice grew soft as he told Jax to stay on the ground. He rested one of his dirt-caked feet on the general's back and let a line of saliva leak out of his pursed lips and onto the back of the general's outstretched head.

Mikalla looked on with a stoic face and a tense heart. He watched as his friend tapped into something Mikalla had never seen before—something evil, crazed. *Oro is cracking, he thought. But why? I can't trust him. But what if he's on my side? Where is this coming from? Maybe he doesn't want this war either... but if that's the case, then who does? Who wants what? There is a force behind Oro—something in the shadows—that I can't control. It's all bigger than me.*

Mikalla's thoughts sped through his mind as he watched the scene unfold in slow motion. *But maybe I can show the people. Maybe I can tell them.*

Oro turned away from Jax and back toward Daniel with a look of icy contempt. "To the dungeon with this one," Oro commanded the guards, "I want him *alive and well*."

Chapter 17

Above all else, Secretary Kitan was a rationalist. Life, to the secretary, was made of springs and gears. They could be left in a pile or scooped up and managed to fit like clockwork. This was the ultimate lens through which he viewed things: pieces to a larger puzzle with no instructions. He reveled in making contraptions out of the cluttered springs and gears of life. A painting, to Kitan, was a collection of brushstrokes that could form a part in a larger mechanism; art was never an end in itself. Kitan was devoted to pragmatism in an almost zealous way. Everything in Kitan's life that failed to serve an end was scrapped, those that served an end were used, and the ends themselves were created, of course, out of innate desires.

As a true pragmatist, Kitan's cups were clay for their grip and cost-effectiveness. As he walked through the narrow hallway in the middle of his bunkered house (a wide hallway would just waste space), he dropped his cup, and it broke on his stone floor.

As he looked down at the wet, shattered clay, he smirked. Unlike when he was out in the political realm, it was a genuine expression—not forced, manufactured, or calculated. The smirk didn't have strings attached, nor was it meant for anyone to see. It came from within himself, from a place of deep self-satisfaction. He softened his gray eyes at the cup. To Kitan, the cheap clay wasn't broken, but rather, transfigured after serving its purpose to its master dutifully and diligently.

Kitan continued down the hall at a lazy pace, and his head tilted to one side after each step. He opened an unassuming door to steps leading down a darkened spiral. He grabbed a torch from the wall and descended into the echoing chamber of his home. The fixtures on the ceiling illuminated a grand table of smooth metal taking up at least half of the whole basement. On the table sat a scale model of the Mesoas Valley, complete with Idaza, Chihopo, and all of the other neighboring tribes and kingdoms. Where there weren't model trees, mountains, or buildings, there were stacks of parchment scrawled with spidery, intricate calculations.

Most of the parchment stacks were multiple feet high, and each sheet was filled with writings, journal entries, ratios, measurements, and blueprints. Everything about the modeled geography—almost to a mundane extent—was incredibly real. Each object's placement was perfect, and the architecture of the different kingdoms mimicked their real forms, as if they were mass-produced toys instead of handmade models. The trees had leaves, the sand had grains, and the people wore the customary garb of the kingdom in which they lived.

Everything was in its place, except for one thing: there were metal tracks weaving through the cities and connecting them, with wheeled vehicles running along the tracks. The vehicles, as Kitan imagined them, held people, mercantile goods, and produce. Some vehicles even held people in a cabin toward the front and a caboose full of maize in the back. It was transport without feet or hooves, commerce for a connected world. What Kitan toiled over was not a region without tribes, but rather, a region where tribes could collaborate through an intricate network of railroads. It was a support system for better commerce, not perfect commerce. The vehicles were shiny and the tracks robust, but there was nothing transcendent about them. There was no mysticism in Kitan's idea of rail transport to unite the tribes of the region. It was simply more advanced. It was better.

Kitan's table model did not depict a utopia. Nor did it display a fantasy. It was simply the world as it was, augmented by Kitan's vision. The wheeled vehicles had a mechanism toward the back operated by two workers who would take turns pushing a lever, hence propelling the vehicle along the tracks. The modeled workers operating the cars matched those of the royal guard hut who constantly lurked around the palace courtyard—they all wore black feathers, black linens, and black-striped faces.

This vision of seamless transportation, in Kitan's eyes, was the most reasonable way to advance the future of the region and, eventually, the world. It was a forward idea that required more than mathematical skill and innovation; it required the largest levers of political and financial power throughout the whole region to be pulled in order to support the resources necessary to make it work. Ultimately, Kitan was not a dreamer. He was a doer, and he would do this or die trying.

Kitan knew it would be costly to execute his vision. And now, with the desperation of King Mirne, the eagerness of General Jax, the incompetence of King Oro, the sycophancy of Tozl, and the ruthlessness of Jani, he had a route to pay for it. There now remained one piece still out of Kitan's puzzle—Mikalla's compliance. If Mikalla were to follow Oro's orders and execute the story well in the ceremony, Kitan would have everything he needed to proceed. He would have everything he needed to control the flow of the mob and unite the region under his transportation system. But he was not completely certain of Mikalla's willingness to abide by rigid orders. Nor was he convinced of Mikalla's aptitude for duty. Always ethereal, never conforming to the status quo of the times, Kitan most hated Mikalla for his independence from the crowd and its frenzied whims. Kitan's power came from his political ability. He could sense a person's emotions and behaviors and read a room like a book. He could see where the tides were turning among people and shift with them. He could, after a brief conversation, know a person's innermost motives, then redirect them to his cause.

Mikalla had to do no such thing to profoundly influence a nation. Unlike Kitan, Mikalla did not look at people as blocks of clay to be sculpted to his desires, but rather to be learned from and admired as finished works of art. All Mikalla had to do in order to embed his visions into the minds of millions was toil over what he loved and craft a seductive experience. He was given the key to the heart of Idaza, and he didn't have to maneuver politically, nor did he have to ascend with sharp ruthlessness. What frustrated Kitan about Mikalla the most was that his pure heart was the reason for his success.

Kitan yearned for a mobile, more cohesive Mesoas Valley. If the nearby leaders were too shortsighted to set aside their petty squabbles, that was their prerogative. He knew people like Oro and Mirne appreciated power for the sheer thrill of knowing others fell below them. But to Kitan, power unused was power wasted, and rules that could not be bent were bothersome roadblocks. He wanted to know more and create more, not necessarily *have* more.

Kitan smiled at his system model like a proud father. On the table, the figurines were still, and the wheels didn't turn. However, his head filled in the gaps, and he saw the future so intimately, he felt as though it already existed—if only just for a moment. He picked up a cobalt metallic vehicle off the table and examined it like a love interest. He turned it over in his hand to reveal the undercarriage. Squinting, he grabbed a scruff of his pressed black robe to wipe the vehicle and turn the clean to the immaculate. He situated the car so its four wheels sat on his palm and brought it up to eye level. He drew a deep, audible breath that started in his emaciated gut then hissed out of his cracked, pale lips. Kitan, with soft eyes and teeth showing, muttered, "The people will finance it, I will control it, and the valley will be *enriched*. We can stop this decay once and for all."

He paced like a windup toy released on the ground. "Seamless. Seamless. Seamless travel. Seamless commerce. No rifts. No dissonance." He paused and halted his compulsive pacing, straightening his hunched vertebrae and lifting his chin toward the ceiling. "It's time for a faster future. And I'll control... it... all."

As his voice trailed off and he drew a sigh, he heard a rhythmic, soft scratching grow louder as it came down the chamber stairs. The warm smirk reappeared on Kitan's face, and he squatted toward the staircase. A scraggly, mop-like dog plodded over to him. From the parts of its eyes not covered in tangled hair, one could sense old wisdom after an exhausting life, as well as a deep and careful contentment. It had a sweeping tail that wagged like a clock pendulum and gray hairs surrounding its long, dry snout. It yawned and revealed missing teeth while it extended its front two legs into a lazy, rigid stretch.

Kitan stretched his arms out to embrace the moppy mutt. "That's a good boy, Jiffy. You're a good dog." He pressed his face to the pet's mangy scruff. "Come on, let's get you fed."

Chapter 18

Mikalla and Jani's backyard was a lush garden grove. It was laced with pinks and purples throughout and had a cooling effect, as if it were a misty lavender haven. Like most of the decor throughout their estate, the garden was Mikalla's brainchild. There was no function to the garden grove. It served no specific purpose. Mikalla constructed it for the sole reason that there was nothing there before. Where many saw dry grass, neglected weeds, and a grub infestation, Mikalla saw a blank canvas. The garden was not a statement, but an art project. It was not meant to be a hangout, nor a workstation, nor a community center. However, if it served to be any of those things naturally, that made its construction all the sweeter for Mikalla's imaginative taste buds.

What Mikalla loved most about creation was its ability to deepen someone's understanding of the world and enrich lives in various ways. That which he sent into the world—as he understood and believed it to be true—was no longer his. In some ways, Mikalla made tools without ever realizing it. A story, painting, or song, or anything else that came from Mikalla, was meant to be received. He was the furthest thing from a utilitarian. In the same token, the utility of enjoyment could not be understated, and Mikalla realized this. Each day, he created and released. So, it was with his flowery enclosure—for it was created, then released to the noble public to be whatever they received it as.

After a morning buried in parchment notes of scriptwriting, Mikalla rubbed his eyes, gave a yawn, and strolled down to the garden for a break after a sleepless night of creative toil. With every stroke of his pen, he couldn't help but picture General Jax on the ground, cooking under the heat of Oro's crazed eyes. It made him uneasy, made him ponder who or what was to blame for behavior like that. He knew Oro was a sensitive soul, and that was part of the reason why Mikalla liked him. What he couldn't figure out, though, was what was hurting and confusing Oro so much as to drive him to an action that grotesque? Was Mikalla next? Was Oro completely unhinged? And if so, who was most influencing that descent into madness? Mikalla went to the garden in the sun to hide from those thoughts for a while.

He opened the door to sunlight and flashes of that pink and purple he so enjoyed. He found cool, sheltered relief under a flowery canvas and took a seat. Twenty feet away, an older woman sat with legs crossed between two hibiscus bushes. She wore a jeweled, lacy cardigan with a silver headband and a diamond ring the size of a raspberry.

Mikalla smiled at the old woman enjoying his creation. When his creative process became arduous after long hours spent scripting and drawing, he refueled his vigor by basking in the experiences he was able to bestow unto others. Although it was Jani's idea in the first place, he enjoyed having a backyard open to the nobles around the Inner Gardens for this reason. Their pleasure in his garden experience was his delight.

"Hello, Ms. Pontigraf; it's a lovely afternoon, is it not?" Mikalla said. The corners of his lips seemed to wrap around his face as he beamed in the speckled sunlight sprinkled across the manicured ground.

The old lady whipped her head so fast toward Mikalla, her earrings clattered. She shot him a reptilian glare that seared through his now-sunken face. He leaned back in his seat instinctively, as if an arrow had whizzed by his head.

"Shouldn't you be *working*?" she spat.

Mikalla now had his hands toward his mouth, and his spine curved into a hunch. He shuddered. "Umm... uh, I'm..." While he stammered, the lady never broke her razor-sharp gaze. The same woman who was on Mikalla's property, delighting in his backyard artisanship, made Mikalla feel as though he were unwelcome in his own place—an outsider in the only land he knew. He was then made a guest in his own creation; he was a stranger in a foreign land, owning nothing and knowing nothing. Ms. Pontigraf had her dark, wrinkled lips pursed and her brow furrowed. She was like a fearless snake staring at its prey. She had every right to encroach, pry, and insult. In fact, her dominance over Mikalla was her sustenance, like a mouse to a cold-blooded serpent.

"I'm taking a break," Mikalla said after a long pause.

At this, the old lady stood up. Her flowing cardigan fell to a natural length, and her eyebrows lifted to more of an accusatory condescension. She was now a parent to a child. "Does Jani know you're doing this?"

"What?"

"I *said*," Ms. Pontigraf's voice simmered in a stew of vitriol and annoyance, "does Jani know that you, the *almighty* Conjurer, are taking a *break*?"

Mikalla stood up and placed his hands on his hips. "Ms. Pontigraf, I don't appreciate your tone, and I really don't know what you mean by—"

"She and the rest better not find out," she huffed.

"Can you please tell me what you mean by that?" he said. As soon as his words were hanging in the air, she was already halfway out of the garden.

Mikalla's chest felt heavy, and his legs became straw. He lay back down to calm his racing heart. He rolled his head onto his cheek in the dirt, and his nervous sweat caked a muddy layer on one side of his face as he lay in a delirious state.

"Jani," he said under his breath. His eyes closed like guillotines dropping, and just like that, he drifted into a cloudy trance. Colors began to whoosh and blur, and the daylight faded from his blurred perception.

***

Mikalla awoke to blue skies and the vast horizon of the ceremony stadium at Mount Chuxat. This was where his crew would do dry runs and dress rehearsals before the ceremony, except his crew was nowhere to be seen. He was alone on his platform, facing the flat slab of the projection rock. He stood where he always did: right in front of the projection pyre. Where he would normally gaze down from his platform and see countless flickering faces, entranced and engaged, he now overlooked a desert of empty stone bleachers as far as his eyes could see. The stadium was so cavernous that even his breath echoed. The misty horizon from hundreds of miles away seemed to be within Mikalla's immediate grasp. He spanned his arms out and lifted his palms toward the balmy blue sky, but the effect seemed to be lost on him. Then, he heard a voice.

"Miki?"

It was Jani.

"Hi, Jani." Mikalla turned to greet her. What his eyes saw nearly made his heart burst. It was Jani, in all of her sultry beauty. She wore a tight black dress and was enveloped in her usual gold accessories from head to toe. Her hair was flowing and full, her lips were large and welcoming, and her sharp, pretty face sat on narrow shoulders. Everything about Jani that was beautiful was dialed up to a ten, except for her eyes. Her eyes were glowing red and shrunken into her face like her brain was a vacuum. She had no pupils, no irises, and no lashes. Her eyes were endless, crimson voids. Her blinking was the only thing that made her seem more human.

"Mikalla. Listen to your heart, Mikalla. You know deep down, don't you? You know who I am," Jani said. Her voice echoed not from the acoustics of the stadium, but from a supernatural source that oozed malevolence. It was as if she had five strident voices instead of one. It wrapped around Mikalla's ears. It jolted his brain and shook the core of who he was, or at least, who he *thought* he was.

He was shocked, disturbed. Yet, somewhere within him, he recognized this Jani. There was a familiarity in those blistering eyes that Mikalla understood. Now, as Jani trekked over to him, he was frozen. His muscles seized.

"I am who I am," Mikalla said. He gritted his teeth. He struggled to hold his gaze on Jani but couldn't stop from blinking repeatedly. "And I know who you are. I love you, Jani."

At that, Jani quickened her stride toward him.

Mikalla gave in. His right foot caved and shrunk back behind him, leaving his left leg extended with all of his weight on his heels.

Jani began running. She was forty feet away and gaining.

Mikalla stumbled back and landed on the rocky platform. He was like a child, a puppy, a clumsy newborn spider scrambling to save himself.

Jani leered at him. She reached under her black dress and pulled out a dagger. Mikalla instantly recognized it as one of Jani's family heirlooms—one typically encased above the headboard in their master bedroom. Stemming from its etched mahogany handle was a shimmering obsidian blade in the shape of a lightning bolt. It tapered off toward the end to form a devastating point. Jani barreled toward Mikalla with the sole intent of slicing and mangling.

Mikalla sat up, staring at her.

Jani came closer. Thirty feet. Twenty-five feet away.

Mikalla desperately scuttled backward toward the ledge. He looked out over the vast stadium. All he saw was an unforgiving wasteland of carved stone. The mountainous bleachers were no longer jagged. The benches were smoothed over after decades of captive rears getting fed Idaza's version of the truth. But what was thought to be Idaza's truth was really Mikalla's truth, and the truths of the many Conjurers before him. What Jani and Kitan understood deeply about him and his work was lost on the rest of the nobles. The lore of Idaza—its history, its mythos, and its *soul*—was funneled through Mikalla and his predecessors. Every pebble in the commons, every child's game, cargo transport, family meal, metalworker's sweaty brow—all were contextualized by him. The myths of the entire kingdom, the gears of its wars, the glory of its history, and the output of its weary labor force all rested on a tightrope of frayed twine.

Jani growled and sneered and slobbered. Fifteen feet. Ten feet away.

Mikalla tensed his forearms and calves. He was now just an impulse.

Five feet.

Mikalla eyed the vastness of the stadium one more time over the ledge of the projection rock. This was where he proliferated, on the grandest scale, countless seeds from himself. He had one human son named Coyote and billions of progenies created here in this stadium. If he died here, he would lie in a grave where so many of his offspring had been born. He recognized the cycle, and there was something now that made sense to him. He jumped and heard Jani shrill.

In a freefall, he was a rock. He cut through the air yet felt motionless. Jani approached the edge from above and looked down at him with pity, disdain, and a kind of toxic satisfaction.

Her eyes glowed and pulsated. Mikalla looked up at her. He wore no expression. His body was resigned, falling into a comatose acceptance. He'd jumped to avoid the plunge of the dagger but was even happier that he'd escaped the red void of her soulless eyes. Then, he braced for impact.

He opened his eyes. He had warm dirt caked on his face.

The midday sunshine nuzzled his body, and the speckled shadows from before were far less pronounced in the garden. Mikalla shuddered and widened his eyes. Sweat soaked his yellow tunic, which was now, much like his face, spattered with a steamy dirt soup. He sat up and wiped the pebbles off his knees. Cool air from the grove filled his lungs as he rose to his feet. It was too fast—he folded back to one knee after a vicious head rush made his vision a purple-and-black kaleidoscope. He clutched his chest, took a gathering breath, and cautiously rose to his feet a second time. His garden grove was vacant now, but he shivered at the thought of how many gilded passersby had caught him sleeping on the dirt in his backyard, drenched in sweat. For Mikalla, there was nothing to be embarrassed about. Nevertheless, there now was something to be scared of. Where that fear came from exactly, he didn't know.

He moved toward the house for a cold shower. The feeling of scrutinizing eyes fell upon him. He was being watched but didn't know by whom. There was no one in sight, but he quickly tiptoed through the grove. His eyes continued to dart around all through his house and up to their master suite. Halfway to the washroom, he spotted the cased dagger out of the corner of his eye, in a glass box disproportionately large for its size. It was layered in a veneer polish, left untouched. Mikalla itched his palms and exhaled slowly.

Jani's family crest was engraved flawlessly into the cherry wood base the knife holder sat upon. The crest was crimson and gold, and at its center was a bald eagle, bold, sharp, and facing sideways. It may have been imposing, and it may have represented something integral to power itself. However, it mattered exactly as much as its controlling family enabled it to. The weight of the crest sat on top of the political and financial capital its members wielded and the maneuverings they pulled. It meant as much as people thought it meant—what people *believed* it meant. And Mikalla could make it mean so little. Mikalla could grasp it in his hand like a slab of meat and toss it into a pit of ravenous wolves. At that thought, he straightened up and continued toward the shower, still tiptoeing.

The filthy tunic was tossed into his and Jani's hamper—the servants would take care of it from there. Crisp water ran down Mikalla's body, taking clumps of brown and gray grime with it. The warm embrace of the sun coupled with the chilling water brought Mikalla back to a workable balance. It was often in the shower where Mikalla did his best thinking; it was where he could prioritize and choose to surface only the most pressing matters.

In his pondering, one question stood out from the rest and clung onto his headspace: *Where is Jani?*

Chapter 19

The beads of sweat across Oro's face grew larger as the night grew colder. He walked quickly through the pillared halls and made a compulsive stop at the cellar of barrels and bottles. With ferocious speed and dexterity, he popped a cork and let the maroon potion drain away the sorrows of the day. The red wine sped him up and slowed down the world; it granted him the calm that had escaped him in the courtyard. Doused with the red potion, Oro then saw the world through a smoother, more viscous lens. The shapes around him took a more fluid form.

A knock from the door above broke the calm of the dim cellar.

"Your Majesty, your sundown appointment is here. Where would you like him to be sent?" a nasal voice asked.

"The council chamber," Oro said. On command, the nasal voice left, and scuttling footsteps faded from above. Oro put his hands to his face and sniffled. He gulped down the rest of his glass then drained the bottle in a few eager swigs. His knees eased their wobbling, his hands stopped shaking, and for a brief moment, he even cracked a soft smile.

On his way to the council chamber, he stopped in a parlor to saturate his mouth and underarms with Idazan-grown mint. With the menthol plant still packed in his cheeks like a nervous squirrel, he beckoned for a servant to fetch a wine barrel for the meeting, then continued on his way.

The council chamber was the highest point in the palace and, therefore, the kingdom. Windows circled the vaulted room, providing a panorama of Idaza available nowhere else. The central meeting table was surrounded by spears—some battle-torn, others new, some silver, others feathered—hung all around. The table itself was circular and had an intricate map of the Mesoas Valley etched on top. There was a metal torch hung directly above the table, providing sufficient light to the rest of the room.

Oro entered up the stairs to find two servants placing down the wine barrel. Two jeweled goblets sat on the map table, glittering in the torchlight from above. One sat in front of the king's chair, which was pulled out in preparation for Oro, and the other goblet was situated directly across from him. Arachnid fingers wrapped around the chalice and lifted it to the lips of a long-faced man. It was Secretary Kitan.

"Good evening, your graciousness."

"Good evening to you, Kitan," Oro said, his mouth creased wide and flat. He sat down. "So, what needs to be done, and what news do you have?"

"Your Highness, the tax collection committee has been chosen and vetted. Everything is now officially in place to receive and allocate funds. In the process, I will emphasize... *expedience*."

"Good." The bulky king let out a belch. "Excuse me for that. I think I had too much fish for lunch." He patted his stomach and chuckled. "That's very good, though."

"Indeed. We are nearing the annihilation of Chihopo. Everything is going as planned…" Kitan trailed off.

"Very well, then. I trust you to make the right decisions here. If you say everything is in place, then I expect it to be. It's as simple as that."

"Well—"

"Well, what?"

"Your Highness, there… there seems to be one small hiccup remaining in the works."

Oro took another swig of wine. "And what is that?"

"Well…" Kitan lifted his thin, serpentine eyebrows. "It's Mikalla."

Oro leaned forward at the mention of Mikalla's name. He furrowed his brow and tilted his head, eyes locked with Kitan's. His hands moved from the goblet and clasped into a fisted ball as he grated his bottom lip under his front teeth. There was no more mint to be smelled from his breath and no more softness in his big, brown eyes.

"What do you mean by that, Secretary?"

Kitan was unfazed and unmoved by Oro's visceral reaction. "There is no intention nor pleasure in me being the bearer of bad news, Your Holiness. Frankly, I was just as disappointed as you're about to be. I bring this to you as your servant. Nothing else."

Oro closed his eyes as if to shield his mind. "I need to know."

"Your Majesty," Kitan said, "Mikalla is acting… *independently*."

"What do you mean by that?" Oro leaned closer still.

"I heard everything from Jani, Your Highness—"

"Get to it, then."

Kitan sighed, attempting to seem broken up about delivering this message. "Mikalla was caught in a state of delirium, sleeping in the dirt in his backyard at midday."

King Oro relaxed his shoulders and puffed out some air. He hiccupped before responding. "Well, that could just be his process. You know how he is. He kind of plays by his own rules, ya know? Not to worry. He'll be ready for the ceremony—I already briefed him," Oro said, nodding to himself.

Kitan pursed his lips and lowered his eyes. "Your Majesty, that's not it. While Mikalla was passed out in his garden, Jani caught a glimpse of the script he's been working on…"

"And?"

"She copied it on a separate page, and… well, why don't I read you the excerpt?" Kitan said, pulling a scraggly piece of parchment out of his sleeve.

"Let me see that." Oro thrust his arm across the table and tugged the parchment from Kitan. Kitan's eyebrows worked hard to suppress his satisfaction.

Oro squinted at Mikalla's introduction. The king was stone-faced as he tore through the parchment, line by line. He stopped every couple of seconds to grunt or hiccup or pose a question to Kitan. "And this was copied *exactly* as Mikalla wrote it?" Oro looked up at Kitan with narrowed eyes.

"I'm afraid so, Your Majesty. Only two nights before the ceremony."

Oro reeled at the words—they were daggers with toxic teeth, injecting despair into his veins. His eyes couldn't graze over the cursed parchment another time—he knew what he'd read, and he couldn't bear to read it again. *The king of Idaza who ate firstborn children… the Chihopo people as small, skinny creatures who cared for their children and worshipped our gods… the Idazan military glorifying sex slavery? This is a trick—a cruel, unnecessary play. A mockery of me, the king fumed. As if my job isn't hard enough.*

Oro put the parchment down and dragged his hands down his fleshy face, stretching his eyelids. He slammed his fist on the table, and his full goblet toppled over onto the map. Wine flowed from the jeweled cup, and soon, the Kingdom of Idaza was enveloped in a sea of blood red.

"Bring Mikalla in. But before you do, I need to take a walk."

"Is everything alright, Your Majesty? You look peaked. I can have a servant fetch you som—"

"Not necessary. I'm fine." With that, Oro excused himself for a break.

He lumbered out toward the royal courtyard, pacing, then stopping to gaze at his reflection after every few steps. His right hand was on his face, rubbing across his lips compulsively. His left hand was fixed to his bulbous hip, unmoving. He was a broad man who, at that moment, seemed small and nervous—a king in his own courtyard who, instead of looking as though he stood atop the world, seemed as though the world was moments from crushing him. The quivering king was at a loss.

Oro had no use for managing perceptions among palace guards and commoners who had no say in anything. Looking regal, to Oro, was not the same as *being* regal. After all, a king can look and act and do what he wants, until he no longer can. What may have seemed like complacent behavior to someone else was both instinctual and trivial to King Oro. He knew no other way and, worse yet, expected no other way than to speak and act as he pleased at any given time. His heart was too large for calculated distrust, and it throbbed too heavily to create emotional distance, *especially* from his closest advisers.

The sky turned a dusky purple with soft orange streaks. Soon enough, it would melt into a black night, at which point Oro would expect his scheduled meeting to commence. His eyelid twitched as he peered up at the sky. Although the air grew crisp at dusk, Oro had beads of sweat running down his forehead. His mind moved at a rapid, sloppy rate, scorning everything and anything that came near. *He's Mikalla the moralist now, huh? Why would he ever do this?*

Mikalla had never harmed anyone before and had always been one of the most generous nobles. But now, he was making Oro's job infinitely more difficult. The king slowly realized there was no way to win—there never was. *What does a legacy mean when it's balanced on a pile of innocent bodies?* he thought, raking his hands through his hair. *Brother... why?*

Oro's racing thoughts were choppy and incomplete, drowned by feelings and nostalgia, singed by competing motivations of legacy, friendship, and a vague sense of piety, and numbed by a strong wave of alcohol. His weary, childish attention was yanked in too many directions to make one right choice, all the while anchored to the face of his father—the ever-disappointed, sharp-eyed, strong-jawed figure that spurred Oro's indecision, his lifetime of inaction. The cold, stoic face of his father was the force that made his entire body tremble. And his friend from way back—the one he could trust, who had liked him for who he was—was making it *more* difficult on him.

But the worst part of all of this was Oro's own nagging doubts: *I can't actually blame Mikalla for not wanting to carry through his task.*

He quickened his pace and scratched his neck compulsively. A weak-legged servant drew nearer with a platter and a glass.

"Fresh water, Your Highness."

"Water? I didn't ask for water. Huh?" Oro said. His eyes caught fire, and he rounded on the frozen servant, whose mouth hung open at the king's harsh tone. Oro stomped across the manicured grass with his large, boot-like feet.

"I—I'm sorry, Your Highness. It—it will not happen again, Your Majesty," the servant squeaked, stammering and cracking through every word. He was now kneeling on the grass toward Oro with his head facing down and his eyes squeezed shut.

Oro kept stomping. His nostrils flared, and his searing eyes were fixed on the boy.

The king swung as soon as he was close enough to strike, sending the tray and glass flying out of the boy's hand with fury. The tray toppled onto the grass, lying flat and unscathed. The glass wasn't so lucky; it was propelled so far by Oro's massive strike that it landed on a stone bed and immediately shattered to bits. If there wasn't silence in the courtyard before, there surely was now. The guards and servants and other attendants in the area pretended not to have seen or heard the incident, but they all stiffened at the weight of the tense atmosphere.

Oro wasn't done. His torrent of emotions had built to a fever pitch. The king's act of disgust fed the conflict within him. His anger doubled, and for the next moment, his vision went red as his consciousness left his body. He took his bearish hands and, after swiping the tray and glass, grabbed the still-kneeling boy by his neck and yanked him to his feet, up to eye level. Oro's yellowed teeth were clenched so tightly together, it was a wonder they didn't crack.

"Who do you think you're fooling? Huh? You're scum!" He raised his fist and—with a sloppy, off-balance strike—punched the skinny servant boy in the nose. Although there was no proper technique to Oro's stroke, the sheer force of the king's size and strength rag-dolled the servant to the ground as his eyes rolled back in his head. Crimson flowed from his face, yet his limp hands were too weak to relieve his nose of the blood.

Oro looked down at the unconscious boy. He glanced toward the shattered glass and the discarded tray then turned away, crossed his arms, and exhaled.

"Away with this mess," the king said, motioning to the boy. He strode off toward his chambers then, shortly after, to the council room—where Mikalla would meet them soon. Oro looked down at his hands in a haze, nearly running. Never again would those hands be useful; they'd never been. It was all a façade, and even his own body was in on the lie.

Chapter 20

"The massacre needs more cymbals!" Mikalla said, snatching the instruments out of the hands of one of his crew members. Mikalla bent his knees when he emphasized his point, as if the words weighed him down as he spoke. His brow caved toward his eyes, and his toothy mouth was spread wide. "This is *killing*. Ruthless, unabashed *killing*." He accompanied every third syllable with a cymbal thunderclap for effect, putting his back into every strike. It was a furious show, yet functional enough to drill into the percussionists the appropriate way to play.

"These are children who have parents, mothers who have families, and workers who are just trying to get by," Mikalla said, "and they're getting *slaughtered*. So start playing like it." And with that, Mikalla dropped the cymbals to the ground as he strode away from the percussionist section.

The studio buzzed that night with all of the urgency and excitement a looming ceremony tended to arouse. Determined members of the crew's various sections darted to different corners and groups to verify and coordinate the nuances of the coming production. It was loud but not cacophonous—frenzied, yet organized.

Just then, he heard a voice. "Excuse me, Mikalla." It was Zac. He had to lean forward when he walked to catch up with Mikalla's frantic pace.

"Hey Zac, I need to get to the props section right now. What is it?" Mikalla never broke nor slowed his stride as he walked. He didn't even bother to spare a glance for the bloated bureaucrat.

"Mikalla, you have visitors. It's urgent."

"Tell them I'm busy. I have a story to tell."

"I don't believe you understand, sir. They've come to retrieve you."

"Retrieve *me*?" Mikalla said, his voice flush with contempt. He stopped right in his tracks, and only then did he concern himself with making eye contact with Zac. "Who is retrieving *me*?" he asked, jerking his index finger up toward his face and widening his eyes.

"Guards."

"Sent from whom?"

"King Oro."

At once, the color drained from Mikalla's face. He shuddered.

Zac's mousy cheeks briefly shifted into a vague, triumphant smile. "The guards are this way, Mikalla. Follow me."

As Mikalla was escorted out, he bit his lip and compulsively twisted his fingers. The thoughts racing through his head were frenzied and varied, but they were all overtly negative. "Zac," he said.

"Mm-hmm?"

"Tell the crew to leave the studio for tonight." Mikalla sighed and looked down between the guards' feet. He was a man defeated, but he didn't know what was going on or who was involved.

"And when should I tell them to come back, sir?"

"I don't know."

And that was the truth—Mikalla really knew nothing. All his agency, all his power, was squashed the moment the king summoned him for a meeting. What's Oro so worried about? *He's never been so uptight in the past. It's like he doesn't trust me...* But the king had always relied on him before. There was something behind this—a dark and deadly force Mikalla didn't trust. *Or maybe... it's someone in Oro's ear, making him anxious about me. Tch!*

Mikalla was led out, but before his eyes wasn't the back of the guard's legs nor the halls of his studio as he left. No. His entire attention twitched and focused on the silver edge of Jani's dagger. The shelved weapon, the dainty, sterling menace—it occupied Mikalla's mind when he walked, when he passed through the Inner Gardens, away from his studio and toward the center of power that lay in the beating heart of Idaza.

Chapter 21

The guards, after a long jaunt around the Inner Gardens and through the pillared halls of the palace, brought Mikalla to a set of stairs he'd never seen before. They were at the back of the palace, down a stretch of dimly lit hallway. The windowless corridor was flanked by two even rows of marble busts depicting generals and aristocrats and decision-makers long passed. Mikalla didn't recognize any of them. The busts were white, but the dark of the hallway made them look a shaded gray. On each of their faces was a blank stare, as if the sculptor was petrified to commit to one look or another. These were not the type of people he told stories about. Mikalla painted grandiose scenes of monarchs and gods and big-chested warriors in the clouds and peaks of mountains. These sculptures were career statesmen, hidden from the public at all costs. Sometimes, Mikalla wondered who was really in charge. The king, or the ones closest to the king? The narratives that wove together the hearts of the nation—how did they form, and who really controlled the stories of their civilization?

The stairs were thick slabs of white marble. They approached a walled outlet with a torch fixture situated within. The flame in the wall seemed to beckon Mikalla toward it—it was a pale light, and it drew him like a moth to a candle in the night. The lone flame illuminated a platform that provided a shift in the stone stairs' path. As Mikalla ascended, the light grew, and the heat of the flames blanketed his body. The air grew heavy, and his steps became rigid.

He made it to the top of the stairs. All that stood between him and whatever lay on the other side of power was one last lonely hallway. In contrast to the decorated staircase and regal wing that surrounded it, this last stretch of passage was plain and modest. Everywhere in the royal palace that wasn't pillared and open was ornamented and themed, except for this corridor. Immediately, the contrast from the rest of the castle stoked the trembling fire in the pit of Mikalla's gut. This wasn't a place for the public. This was where the legacies of the nameless marble busts were made. He wasn't summoned to the chamber to discuss his role on the team. As of now, Mikalla belonged to no team. He was a rogue, a target in the eyes of whoever spoke the loudest in Oro's bloated ear.

As much as he may have pitied himself for consistently being an outcast throughout his life, it was he who chosen to act independently, and it was he who had the agency to do so. He'd always had the agency. Mikalla had always been granted a long leash of freedom few others in his society had the privilege of enjoying.

He cared about the fruits of the power in the present. He lived in the present, and he created for it, too. Even the futures Mikalla conceptualized were meant to be lived presently, fully in the moment. To Mikalla, the future was only as good as the quality of the moments it allowed for. Whatever was at the other end of the leash would be unbothered by Mikalla so long as the holder gave him enough cord to roam as he pleased.

While approaching the entrance to the council chamber, he did not know who held his leash. What he did know, however, was that the leash was considerably shorter than he'd realized, stopping him from roaming freely. For Mikalla, this was a problem too large to ignore. This house of cards rested upon too rickety a platform. He thought of Kitan, the one who was always around but never in the middle of the centrifuge. Maybe it was he who controlled the storm; maybe he directed its might at his rivals, all those who stood in his winding way.

Mikalla knocked on the chamber door. It was soft, massive wood—not sanded nor shaved nor carved. He heard nothing.

Another second crawled by. A few long moments later, he heard a whisper on the other side.

Someone cleared their throat audibly. "Come in, Mikalla." It was King Oro.

The screech of the door was the only sound as Mikalla entered the room. A barrel with a spigot—of what Mikalla could only guess was wine—sat next to King Oro. Secretary Kitan was poised so he directly faced the entrance. Satisfaction dripped from his gaunt face, though there was nothing overt about it—there never was. What unnerved Mikalla more was the impression he had that, at any time and under any circumstance, Kitan could be carefully calculating each and every facial expression. The idea that even the slightest eyebrow flick, lip twitch, or head turn could be a manufactured ploy that was *meant* to be displayed gave Mikalla the guttural urge to shudder. It was a shudder he would have to conceal for now, as he had two sets of piercing eyes analyzing his every move. *What value does Kitan add to the king's court? I don't even know what he does on a daily basis.*

Both pairs of eyes scanned Mikalla's face, searching his expression. Mikalla avoided eye contact with both of them at all costs, keeping his hard gaze fixed on the wine-stained table instead and letting his peripheral vision guide him toward his chair. The many spears that encircled the room all seemed to point at Mikalla. It was as if one of them could dislodge itself and barrel through the air like a ghostly projectile at any time, impaling his chest with its silver tip.

"Bow before His Majesty," Kitan ordered. His voice was deep and slow.

Kitan's command, coupled with the newfound dynamic between them, made Mikalla's blood boil. His skin got hot and tingly, and his back tensed. However, even though he was infuriated by his own subordination, he knelt rigidly before his king. To the king, it was a strong show of respect. For Mikalla, it was an act of backward defiance. *Who does Kitan think he is? He's playing some weird power game. But why? What could he want? He's already at the top, right beside the king...*

They each occupied a third of the table, with Oro and Kitan's lines of sight converging on Mikalla, who was now seated. Oro cleared his throat. He sat forward in his chair with his beefy elbows on the table. Kitan perched straight and still. He looked like a predator that had cornered its prey, right before it began chowing down on its latest catch.

Kitan didn't look poised to talk, nor did he have to. There were no more perceptions to manage, no more balls to roll in order to sell his contrived war. Mikalla was his last obstacle to knock down, and as far as he could tell, everything was in place for the pin to fall.

Oro did everything he could to keep a burp from escaping his lips. "So," he started, drawing out his first word, "Mikalla, do you know why you're here?" Oro tilted his round head to one side and clasped his fists together. He scooted back slightly when he spoke.

"I do not, Your Majesty."

At Mikalla's words, Kitan snickered. It was just loud enough for everyone to hear.

"Mikalla, I need you to listen. You will not ask any questions. Just give me answers. Are we clear?"

"Yes, Your Majesty."

"Alright. What was your story about for the ceremony?"

"The shining future of Idaza and the brilliance of victory," Mikalla replied.

Kitan stood from his seat and marched over to fill his goblet underneath the gold spigot, as if just barely listening to Mikalla.

"Mm-hmm," the king said, studying the spilled wine on the table then looking up at the vaulted ceiling. "And what problems do you see with your portrayal of the kingdom?"

"I... do not see a problem, really—"

"*Really*?" Oro interjected. His rancid breath pervaded Mikalla's innocent nostrils. "You don't see a problem, *really*?"

"Really, I don't... Your Majesty." At Mikalla's answer, Kitan fidgeted in his seat.

"There's nothing... *heinous* in it? No slaughter that breaks our warrior code? Nothing that would portray our leadership as... faulty?"

Mikalla's guts leapt to his throat. *How did he find out? What else do they know? Who's the culprit? What do I do? What's going to happen to me? Where can I turn? I shouldn't have done this.*

Mikalla kept his eyes away from Oro's and held his face as straight as he could. To leak even an ounce of emotion would be like feeding oil to a hungry flame. He was bloodied in shark-infested waters, and the bystanders offered no rafts—in fact, to Mikalla's confusion and anguish, they seemed to cheer on the feeding frenzy.

Compliance was only ever just an option to Mikalla, never an end in itself. Compliance was a tool and a *suggestion*. If it worked to support his art, then it would serve as a helpful boon to his work—but it rarely did in any way. Whether or not Mikalla's compliance could have enabled him to avoid this situation all along, he couldn't bring himself to fully place the blame on his own head. There was a deeper-seated change in the tides of influence at the highest level of Idaza. Mikalla still couldn't figure out why or how. What he did understand was there was no room for loose ends in this new paradigm, and to them, he was exactly that: a nonconformist loose end. He was an independent operator who was now cornered in a circular room.

Insults to his art were never problems for Mikalla. They hit him like tiny hail pellets would hit a window. He knew he was talented, and he let his expressions manifest themselves freely through his abilities regardless of what people said. Therefore, it was not insulted work that posed any real threat to Mikalla; it was *stifled* work. The hairs on his neck, the stew in his gut, and the itch in his palms told him there was a fork in the road, and one of the two routes now facing him meant stifling his work to the point of destroying it fully. Instead of using tools to create, he would effectively become one for destruction, for death—the ugly opposite of creation, its abusive older brother. The other path for Mikalla was wrought with far more pain and treachery. It would mean, invariably, an end to his beloved career and almost definitely an agonizing end to his life. Although neither of those options were pleasant, he faced the fork in the road with wolves chomping at the bit. He had to choose one.

It was a shame for Mikalla's career that he couldn't enchant the two nobles in the room the way he did the sea of commoners. He played the only card he felt like he had in his hand at that point.

"Your Majesty," Mikalla started as his eyes swept the room, eventually landing on Oro's forehead, "I have no idea what you're talking about." His mouth formed a strained, straight line after finishing his reply to the king.

Oro was not pleased.

"How do you want to do this, Mikalla? This doesn't have to be difficult."

Mikalla gained a twinge of confidence. In that statement, he felt a familiar piece of Oro—a piece that was warm and personal. It was sympathy for Mikalla. The king knew what was being done and also what could be done to Mikalla, and he felt bad about it—genuinely bad to his fluffy core. The king was trying to give Mikalla an out, and the Conjurer felt, if only for a moment, an emotional tether that was much needed in this dire situation. It could have all been in Mikalla's mixed-up head, or maybe Oro was just drunk. Or it could have been a legitimate shift in the room's atmosphere. Either way, Mikalla was going to try to go with it.

"How could I make this easier on you, Your Highness? All I want to do is help the war effort however I can. If there is an inclination of yours that I am not, please tell me how I could better my standing and my process." Mikalla felt Kitan's pressure, his overwhelming desire. If Kitan could bend Mikalla like hot metal, like one of his many other predictable tools, he would have gladly done so. Kitan just wanted things to make sense—and Mikalla made no sense.

Kitan fidgeted in his seat again. His restlessness poked through the thin, transparent barrier between the three.

"Kitan, anything to add?" Oro prompted.

Kitan ran his hand through his slick, greasy mane. "You need more guidance," he snapped. "And you clearly need more direction. In your script. In your performance. In your story. In your delivery." His tongue was snake-like, pronged and snapping. "This isn't arts and crafts anymore, Mikalla." The two locked eyes with the force of either great rivals or great friends—there was a longing intensity that burned in their stare.

Oro took a deep breath and looked back down at the table. "Mikalla, tomorrow you will submit a new, full-length script with a storyboard attached to be edited and approved by a committee of my choosing. You'll receive a list of mandatory inclusions and rules to follow." Oro hiccupped after the last syllable.

"Yes, Your Highness. It will be done."

Kitan cleared his throat.

"And if your script is not up to a certain standard on your first submission," Oro continued, "then you will be exiled from Idaza permanently." The king looked back up at Mikalla. Oro's eyes were wide, hurt. "I'm sorry to have to do this, Miki."

Kitan knew Oro liked Mikalla, and he knew Mikalla could pull second chances out of the king. *You can't be sorry, Oro. There is nothing you should be sorry for. Nothing.* Kitan looked down at the ground, yet he saw a vision of the future, his future, the best future for the Mesoas Valley. Tracks for transport, kingdoms bound by trade, by modern solutions—not by brute force. This was Kitan's future, where success was gained through wit and grease, handshakes and poison—Kitan's type of game. But then, in Mikalla, he saw a wrench in his plan, the most effective blocker to his dream. He saw his whole world pass by in Mikalla's dreaming eyes and wither away in the blaze of the fool's childish heart.

I need to stop this infant before he goes too far, he thought, narrowing his eyes at the miserable man. *He'll ruin everything. He'll ruin me.* To Kitan, Mikalla's actions could destroy the entire kingdom. He was afraid the Conjurer would ruin them all if he didn't do something about him.

This irresponsible child. Mikalla's feeble mind needs to be bent out of my way... through hell or anything else. Damn Mikalla to a death of sharp metal.

Chapter 22

Mikalla walked back from the palace through the black haze. His steps were sandbag heavy as he trudged back to his house. He was blank and unaware. He could barely see his own footsteps as his vision blurred into the rest of the fog. But that was okay for now, because to be able to see clearly was unfortunately life-affirming. Sharp senses made for a sharp reality, and Mikalla didn't want to be cut any longer, constrained and boxed into a fate chosen by a bureaucrat. He wasn't angry. He was too deflated to harbor any kind of frustration. Anger would've meant he had energy and resolve, two things that had been crushed by the gears of war and the fiends who turned them.

Mikalla walked on through the bleak fog and biting thoughts of the opaque desire behind Kitan's smug face. The heavy night sky weighed down and pressed on his weary shoulders, bending and ready to break.

He'd always thought his riches were somehow a fruit of his labor, a source of freedom he gained by making good art. He then realized his many possessions were a ball and chain. They were imposed by a higher authority, not given or granted. His manor was a golden dungeon, but a dungeon all the same. The leash he thought he had was shorter than he ever could have imagined. He was a siphon and a tool. He was a servant, yet he still didn't know who he served. Maybe it was better for his psyche that he served a faceless shadow instead of a person. Maybe it was Kitan, or maybe it was the king pulling the strings all along. It was impossible to know, yet the questions zapped his tired mind, giving way to the heaviness of chaos, crushing him under the starry sequins of night.

He realized then that the sea of commoners he so often looked upon didn't stand below him. They stood atop him, supported and bound by the stories he conjured. Mikalla had held up the commoners all along. His audience was his pride. And now, he was forced to take from that which he'd raised and shaped in his own image over years of sweat and brilliance, years of sacrifice and thought—all his life's work that begged and clawed and reached for the stars. Under his feeble breath, he whispered, "Are we all just pieces that don't need to be here? Pieces to a puzzle that doesn't need to be finished? Damn it all to hell."

He trudged on to the front door of his vast estate—his golden dungeon.

***

Jani lay in the bed with cloudlike down comforters blanketing her bare body. There were silk garments strewn across the floor. She turned over to the man lying beside her. "You'd better get out of here," she said. Her voice was still a whisper in the dark. The only thing visible in the master suite was the dagger encased above the headboard, reflecting the bleak moonlight from the window. The tranquility of dusk's colored sky had turned to a night of translucent haze. It was a rare fog that beset Idaza that night, the dreary enemy of light.

A sigh and a deep groan came from the man in the bed. He caressed Jani's thigh with his hand. "Maybe not yet," he said in a raspy, hushed voice. His head rested like a sleepy infant on her navel. "Just a little more."

Jani reached out her hand to clasp his. She had a long, slender hand, much like the rest of her sultry body. She removed his hand before bringing it up to her face and kissing it. "No, no more," she said. "You need to leave now."

The man grunted and jerked his body upright. He was a muscular nobleman in his thirties, younger than Mikalla. He slid on his smooth, drab tunic and bent over to kiss her forehead. Jani obliged but didn't move an inch.

"And make sure you do what I told you," Jani whispered, turning away from the man, who was now sliding on his footwear to leave.

***

Mikalla stopped in his front yard to catch the racing breath in his chest. He inhaled cool, indifferent air that stuck to his lungs and throat.

Even with his limited awareness that night, something did strike him as odd: There was no torchlight emanating from his home—not from the kitchen, nor the dining room, nor even the master suite. He brushed this aside and continued toward the front door.

Upon entering, he heard footsteps in the pitch black. His pupils became pinpricks, and his dashing heartbeat returned. He rose up on his toes and balled his fists. "Jani? Coyo? Is that you?"

No response. There was pure quiet as Mikalla stopped in his tracks, trying to locate the sound. "Show yourself! Who's there?" Mikalla scrambled for a torch and dagger. Instead of the black of night, his vision became red with fury.

His heart raced.

At the sound of Mikalla's steps and rustling, the scampering continued, this time farther away from the grand entryway. It was headed for a backyard escape.

His breath hitched. Pupils wide, he sprinted after the footsteps. "Jani! Where's Jani? Hello? Show yourself!" Mikalla yelled. He began throwing ornaments and figurines toward the back of the house, where he heard the footsteps. The shattering of clay and the crashing of bronze only made the shadow's escape into the night easier.

Mikalla scrambled blindly toward the back. He yelled. He heard the pounding steps, the breath of a man unwanted.

His chest heaved.

The breathing got closer, the steps got louder. In the chaos, Mikalla took a wild swing with a large vase. He put his entire might into it, all his force—but he hit air and darkness, nothing else.

And then, like smoke turned to invisible vapor, the stranger slipped away into safety. The footsteps crunched past the glass and squished into the yard, away from certain pain.

After the commotion faded, Coyote's infant voice shrilled from the other room. His crying hurt Mikalla, but it assured his survival. Mikalla bolted into his son's room. The child was balled up in his blankets, sobbing and screaming loudly, his dark eyes streaming tears.

Mikalla lowered his voice to a whisper and took hold of Coyote with both arms. "It's okay, buddy. You're safe now. Everything is fine. It's okay." Coyote's sobbing didn't stop at Mikalla's comforting, but he did quiet down some. At the commotion, Jani walked down the stairs and stood in Coyote's doorway.

"What's going on? I was asleep," she said. Mikalla rushed over to her and wrapped his arms around her. He kissed her on the cheek and realized her makeup was still on from earlier that day.

"Are you okay?" Mikalla asked breathlessly.

"I'm fine. Are *you* okay? Why are you back so early?"

"Jani, someone was *in* our house. I don't know what he did or what he wanted…" Mikalla began to shiver. "Didn't you hear that? Any of that? The crashing? Did you hear me when I came in?"

"Did he make the noise?" Jani asked. She still sounded lethargic and unafraid as she walked over to hug Coyote.

"I tried to get him, Jani. I'll assess the damage later. You guys are okay, though. Oro needs to know about this." Sitting on the bed, he put Coyote on his lap and Jani in his other arm. He embraced them, and they stayed together on the bed as a unit for some time that night.

After a while, Mikalla put the sleeping infant to bed, and Jani tucked him in and kissed his forehead. Mikalla stood up with Jani as they walked through the dark manor. They went to the back of the house, where the damage had been done. A spattering of glass, clay, ceramic, and much else littered the shadowy floor.

"Tomorrow, the servants can take care of it," Jani said as she turned away from the scene and up toward their bedroom. Mikalla rose from his squat and followed closely behind. Jani picked up her pace on the stairs, if only slightly.

"Jani, where were the guards? Why weren't they here?" Mikalla probed. "I mean, this is a huge problem. I need to talk to Jax about it tomorrow, at least Oro—"

"Don't do that," Jani blurted. She turned around to face Mikalla just before the entryway to their master suite.

"What? Why not?" By this point, the calamities that had happened around Mikalla had created a rift in his heart. As his adrenaline melted away, so did his judgment, his vision, his fortitude, and his better thoughts.

"Miki, they're busy enough as is. You wouldn't want to bug them. Not right now, anyway. I'll just request more guards tomorrow. It was a simple lapse—a *mistake*."

"Aren't you going to report this?" Mikalla asked. "Why are you acting so weird?"

"Acting weird? Mikalla, it's the middle of the night, and all I can do right now is sleep." Jani was flippant and quick. "You're the one who's throwing heirlooms at people you don't even know."

At Jani's offhand comment, Mikalla's world went fuzzy again. He didn't have the bodily resolve at that time to be angry. The most he could do was reply in an exasperated tone, like the wounded animal he was. "Jani, what's going on? Seriously, tell me." Mikalla's eyes began to well with tears, and his jaw tensed.

Jani looked him in the eye and stayed still. Mikalla's sharp cheeks reflected the only light present in the house. *He's frantic right now,* Jani thought. *He's starting to ask questions and look around. I need to get him to sleep. Does he know I turned in his script? No. But I bet he's contemplating it—deep in the back of his mind, he's churning that possibility around.* "You're very tired right now, Miki. Let's work this out tomorrow. The mess will still be there."

Mikalla's voice cracked. He shook his head slowly. "Jani, what's going on? I can't handle this right now. Please…"

Jani stared at him, stone-faced, lips pursed, one hand on the doorway.

Silence.

Mikalla strode toward her, keeping eye contact, but Jani stood her ground. *He's a rabid animal right now. I know him like this—not enough sleep, not enough time, not enough space. I need to slow him down.*

"Miki, let's—"

"Tell me!" Mikalla yelled through gritted teeth.

Jani felt a storm, a sea of rage and blood, surge through her veins. Her pet was biting the leash that held him. "Listen, you ungrateful little child, you have no idea how much I do for you or how ridiculous you're acting! You're being a damned fool right now! Now shut up before I make you sleep on the couch—you've been embarrassing me lately!"

They were both in the bedroom at that point, and even with bleary eyes, Mikalla spied a headband he didn't recognize flung on the floor beside their bed. He stomped toward it.

Jani sprang for it, but Mikalla grabbed her feeble wrist and jerked her out of the way so hard she fell backward.

He let out his breath and stood still. Holding up the headband, he let it hang away from his body in a pincer grip for Jani to see. His voice was at a whisper now, and the room was quiet enough for him to hear both of their pounding hearts. "I don't understand," he whispered. But it only took a second for the world to rush in, all of its mountain peaks and writhing snakes of venom. "This is what you think of me?" He shook it around. "Huh?"

"I think it's time for you to go," Jani breathed. She remained on the floor, rubbing her wrist. *I've lost all control. He's on his own now.*

"I think so, too," Mikalla said, dropping the headband before walking through the master suite doorway, back into the darkness.

The only glimmer of any light in that room came from the small shimmer of the silver dagger above their bed. It was Jani's dagger—the same one Mikalla felt twisting and writhing in his chest at that moment. He didn't need to get stabbed by it to feel its cold teeth sink into his skin, to taste the cold metal ripping, burrowing, searing into his soft flesh.

The silver dagger struck without striking. There was never a tear so cold, nor a cut so clean.

Torn through his heart. Stabbed in his back.

Chapter 23

Mikalla went to the only place he could be safe that night. He slid through the back entrance of the studio and lit a torch. At night, alone, the studio was bleak and empty. The deserted theater wasn't very large but seemed to go on forever in the light of his handheld flame. The silence enveloped Mikalla, but he was too tired to get chills or be on alert. He slunk through a back passage and up a narrow flight of stairs to his studio office. Mikalla set the torch down then lit another. During the day, the floor-to-ceiling windows of his office portrayed a scenic view of Idaza's mountain horizon. What was normally a patch of paradise complementing his workspace was now a murky oblivion that seemed to close in on Mikalla the more he stared at it.

A thick stack of parchment sheets, untouched, lay on his desk. The flicker of the flame illuminated a wall of paintings, all of which Mikalla had commissioned at different times throughout his life and career. In contrast to the royal palace's decor, there were no battle scenes or weapons anywhere. The largest painting hung in the middle of one wall. It was a depiction of a peasant laborer—a faceless worker with only a brow line and a straight mouth bending over to harvest maize in a tattered tunic. The sun looked harsh and hot, and it boiled the ground around the toiling peasant. There were paintings of fruit, of gods, fires, mountains, and kings long past. And then, of course, toward the upper corner of the room, there was the portrait of him, Coyote, and Jani looking ahead, each of them smiling with closed lips. He couldn't bear to look at it long. The only thing he wanted to see at that point was oblivion—that would have been his only solace. *I don't doubt Jani turned in my manuscript to the government. I should have known. But how could I have? What could I have done differently? Is this all my fault?*

Mikalla took one sheet of parchment off the top of the stack and, within a minute of sitting down to write, began sobbing uncontrollably. The plant-fiber amate paper was too thin to hold his tears, so he balled it up and threw it against the wall. *Am I the monster or do I just live among them?* His mind was stripped down to only that question. He was sick with anguish, not wanting to move yet needing to go.

He didn't want to be in his own skin. He didn't want to be alive. Everything in him was writhing, yet completely paralyzed. He could barely breathe. There was no depth of loneliness darker nor more abiding. There was no limit, no stopping point, to his descent. *They're all liars. Every last one of them. Everyone. What is left for me?*

The only thing that felt natural at that moment was curling up into a fetal ball on the ground and letting his tears flow. The warmth of the torch was his only refuge on the cold office floor. He took a few more sheets of parchment, balled them up, and used them as a pillow. *What will Coyote do?* And below even the deepest pretensions of his mind, a conclusion pierced him, making him heave, writhe, and burn inside: *She has the power to wrestle him away. And what's stopping her now? My son...* the one who looked up at me with those big eyes and loved me for who I was—not for what I did or who I knew, but for me. *My son...*

He stared out the black window through red, weary eyes, wishing the void would swallow him. He didn't want a new start; he wanted an end.

Chapter 24

Secretary Kitan seldom stepped outside of the capital. On the rare occasions he did, he took a shadowy back route, tucked away from the commotion of the commoners, surrounded by his regular enclave of guards. The lush vibrance of the city turned to a flat, rocky desert.

He walked toward a lone building in the distance. It was larger than a hut but smaller than a temple, and it looked like a giant stone box. It had no windows and multiple chimneys. The closer Kitan got, the louder the noises from inside the building became. There was hammering, smelting, bantering, and whirring about. At the entrance, the secretary was greeted by a thin man in a fibrous mask wearing a brown canvas sheet that enveloped his body. The man took off his mask to kneel and formally greeted Kitan. His face was far longer and narrower than those of most of the people in Idaza, and he wore a constrained but warm smile.

"Please," Kitan said, "it's only been a few moons. Don't kneel for me, Director."

"As you wish, sir." The man grinned. His teeth were straight and honest, his voice nasal. "You're going to like what we have to show you, Secretary."

"I'm sure I will, Max," Kitan said, letting out a quick laugh and nodding slowly.

They walked in while the black-clad men stayed outside to guard the entryway. At once, the presence of Kitan hushed the building. The workers turned to face the secretary. Kitan acknowledged them with a passing glance and continued through the main corridor, with the director leading the way. There were metal scraps, planks of wood, and wedges everywhere. Kitan was less concerned with the parts and more with the whole of what they would become.

"Right this way," the director said, stretching out his arm. They stood in front of a thick stone wall with one door blocked by straw and sticks. Kitan fanned them out and ducked through the makeshift portal. What he saw on the other side made him gasp. His long jaw dropped open, and his eyes widened.

"Well, here's the prototype, sir," Max announced with his hands on his hips. "Just finished this morning."

Kitan swallowed. He saw the vehicle that matched his table models with striking accuracy, wheels and all, only he could *sit* in it. He slapped the director on the back and laughed as if it were a joke, except it was all too real. After touring and inspecting every inch for what seemed like a day, Max walked him upstairs to a small parlor with a seating area and ready-made cups of juice.

The secretary exhaled and sat down, taking a hearty swig of the drink. "Max, I'm thoroughly impressed... My vision is *alive*." His eyes lit up at the last word.

"I mean, you thought of it, sir. We just materialized your plan." Max eyed the cup and didn't drink. He sat rigidly in the chair despite the praise. He then looked down at the ground.

"So, how do we proceed, Director? Are we still on schedule for testing?"

Max straightened his torso, still rigid in his seat. He bit his lip and continued to eye the floor, shuffling his feet. "Well, there is one thing, sir."

Kitan raised his eyebrows. "And that is...?"

"Well." Max stroked his chin. "We need more funds... and soon."

Kitan drained the short-lived cup of juice. "I'm taking care of that right now," he said, standing up with his hands behind his back. "Soon enough, we won't just have the money to test, but we'll be able to *scale*, Director."

Max itched the back of his head, unconvinced. "Sir, this is getting, well, *expensive*."

Kitan walked over to the director. Bending down, he locked eyes with the man and raised his eyebrows. "Max, I'll soon have the money not just for the next phase, but for the whole of this project. *I'll* worry about the funds. And you," his voice grew lower, "you worry about your job."

Chapter 25

Oro laughed at Jani's joke. They sat in an annex of the palace, away from the open halls and the scuttling of servant feet. The king patted his round gut and ran two of his fingers across his forehead. His yellowed teeth showed. "Ah, you've always known how to take me out of a bad mood, Jan."

"Just like old times," she said, sipping from her goblet. She put the drink down and looked back at him. "Why were you in a bad mood in the first place, though? I know times may be a little tough right now, but I just want you to be happy, Oro."

The king looked away. "Yeah, well, I appreciate that, and I appreciate your company this morning. Sometimes, even a king needs a break." He stretched out his arms. "And I hate to say this, but I need to go right now. I've got a kingdom to wrangle."

"Okay, then," Jani said, "but do you mind waiting one second? I need to tell you something."

"Of course," he said. "Oh, how is Mikalla doing, by the way?" It was a quick question the king posed carefully. He fidgeted as the air became heavier on his shoulders.

"Well," Jani sighed, "that's what I was going to bring up."

Oro leaned forward and stared at Jani, studying her every move. "Mm-hmm?"

"Oro, it kills me to say this, but it hurts more to keep it inside: I think Mikalla is going crazy."

The king let out a weak chuckle and looked back down at his toes. "Jani, he's always been a little crazy."

"You don't understand. He's... he's *descending*."

"Jani," the king said, lowering his voice and leaning in farther for emphasis, "he has a *lot* of pressure on him. Yes, he *has* been hard to manage. But Jani, he's coming up on the biggest ceremony of his life, and I'm asking him to do things he's never had to do before. What he needs right now is sp—"

Jani shot up a bit, feeling the control of the conversation begin to melt through her sharp nails. Oro's perception of Mikalla was more steadfast than she'd thought. Now, Oro had to be overcome by force, not just contorted by careful claws. She felt her calves tense from her chair as she narrowed her eyes into a snake-like stare. "*No*, Oro, you ar—"

"Don't interrupt me." The king clobbered the table with his balled fist. "Don't... Jani." Oro clenched his surly jaw and, now unprovoked, seemed to get angrier. His fist bashed the table again with full force. A glass on a nearby shelf fell and shattered from the tremor. "You listen to me. All Mikalla's ever done is serve this kingdom with *loyalty*... and *grace*!" The king's nostrils flared, and he had venom in his eyes. "And all I've done is put him in increasingly difficult situations. And it's because my hand has been forced as well—all of ours have. I know that script was awful. But now he's changing it." Oro raked his hands down his face. "So, problem solved, then."

"Yes, Your Majesty. I understand," Jani said. She was stone-faced and still, with her mouth slightly open. Every fiber within her was tensed and focused; her single intent was to contort, with wispy, probing, wiry means, Oro's perception of Mikalla. She *couldn't* be the bad guy, she *couldn't* be the oppressor, the miser, the wrongdoer. It was Mikalla who was the crazy one, and she had to prove it to absolve herself of cheating on the king's friend, the divine Conjurer. She already knew she was in the right; she always had been, ever since she was little. But Oro was staying strong in his convictions, too emotional to waver.

"Do you? Do you understand? Because I have the weight of the kingdom on my back, and it's maddening! Okay? Honestly—who can I rely on completely? Hm?" The king sat back, took a deep breath, and wiped the sweat from his brow. An animalistic anger flashed across his face then left in the same instant.

"Oro," Jani said softly in a velvet whisper, "you rely on me, you can count on me... You know that. Of course you can. Don't—why are you shaking your head?" *He's out of his mind right now, too emotional to judge anything for himself... but then again, he's always been that way.*

"Everyone wants something different, Jani. Mikalla, Kitan, and the rest. I just can't figure out what it is everyone wants. But they all conflict—every last one of them. It's all a mess."

Jani stared down, far down, at the king—like a parent to a child. "I don't want something different than what you want—it's all for the kingdom. I want what's best for Idaza. That's it."

"You're not stupid, Jani. But do you think *I* am?"

I can't let him walk all over me, Jani thought. "Why would you ask such a thing?"

"Because you're acting like I'm stupid."

"And why do you think that?"

"You're talking like I have agency, like I can control what's going on."

Half under her hot breath, she muttered, "Well, you *are* the king."

"Yes, Jani, and I have a job, too."

As they departed the room, the toxic, knowing tendrils within Jani took hold and spread their story. They told her the truth, the reality she didn't want to face but had to see—had to look in its white eyes. She felt—and more so, she *knew*—that Oro was half-hearted. She knew his allegiance to Mikalla was too strong and his convictions were too soft to side with her for long. *He's nothing but some clown, some woven bag that blows with the wind.* She loathed how quickly his emotions could dissipate, then spring up anew somewhere else like a geyser. *Kind of like Mikalla*, she considered, *both of them just grown children. I guess the most powerful among us are the most pathetic. Disgusting.*

She walked out of the palace and into the light of the barren day, the dry air, the blank sky. *Something will have to be done.*

Chapter 26

G eneral Jax stood as a resolute statue, hands behind his back, watching his men march to and fro. He inhaled the hot, dry air and basked in the whirring of the working warriors scattered about the stadium. They were setting up camp in and around the stone amphitheater at Mount Chuxat the day before the ceremony. It was to ensure that positions and procedures were met correctly before the crowds arrived. For every ceremony Idaza held, there were guards and armed warriors watching over the event. At this ceremony in particular, there would be an uptick in military involvement, as commanded by Kitan, and Jax was there to make sure things went smoothly.

"Sir, a moment?" A tall man with an athletic build approached Jax. He was dressed in a tunic that stuck tightly to his chiseled upper body. Bands circled his ankles and wrists, and he had a scar that ran the length of his face.

Jax turned toward the man, then escorted him to a nearby guard hut set up at the base of Mount Chuxat. Spears of all shapes and sizes lined the back wall of the hut, and they both sat down in front of them. "Sir, we have the south face secured, and everything will be buttoned up around the perimeter. We'll have two cohorts patrolling the crowd, and—"

"Make that three," Jax said.

"Yes, sir. I will get on that. But besides adding that cohort, everything seems to be sealed tight and compliant. I'm looking for the 'okay' from you to send my men on break for this afternoon."

Jax cleared his throat. "Okay then, I'll give it a once-over." He held up his hand and started marking each of his fingers, starting with his index. "But if you call me out there and I see a hiccup anywhere—the perimeter, the crowd, the stage, the pyre, the crew stable, the entrance, anywhere at all—then it'll be bad news for you, Commander."

The muscled man got up and shook Jax's hand with violent fervor. "Thank you, sir. My men have been diligent all day. I can promise you that."

Jax looked out over it all; a dark shadow descended upon the theater as a determined cloud smothered the infant sun. It hung over all of them, thick and large, enveloping the general's head in a shadowed vise grip.

Chapter 27

Mikalla's raccoon eyes revealed a glimpse of his exhausted soul. By midmorning of the next day, he'd composed a drafted script worthy of nothing except the eyes of a fool. But the script would suffice because that was all he made it to do. It would pass right under the nose of King Oro and even get the stamp of approval from Secretary Kitan—Mikalla knew that to be true. He left it with a crew member to submit to the king, then hobbled back up to his office to gather himself. His head was a tangle of nonsensical thoughts whizzing by, drawing blood as they passed. Although his body ached and his reasoning was dull, his anxieties were sharp and heavy. His awareness of the future was obscure. He was starting to believe he didn't have a future at all—a creeping and heavy notion that seeped into and enraptured his being. That acute, black despair was everywhere, tightening its grip every minute he stayed alive, fighting—and losing—his existential struggle.

He was stuck between states of over-heightened awareness and a complete lack of it altogether. He didn't feel trapped, but he wished he could. At least if he were back trapped in his golden prison, he could be fed, safe, and cared for. He could have tools and toys and a childish type of freedom he hadn't known he craved until he lost it. Being trapped was, at that moment, a luxury.

The world as he knew it collapsed on him with ferocious speed and violence. Being trapped in mind-numbing opulence and interpersonal bliss would have been a haven from this horror. He was always okay with his life being controlled by the whims and needs of all sorts of other people. He always understood that other people and obligations, as bothersome as some may have been at times, were necessary tethers to an outside world that fed his creation and enriched his life. But now, he was a man untethered.

He discovered that, when stripped of everything, all that was left at his core was art—creations, depictions, reflections, expressions. Art was his defiance—his rebellion against the ornery whims of the people, the betrayals, and the subterfuge of the fickle crowds throughout his short life—against that which he couldn't control. Art, creating characters, and expressing the elation and pain of life—*that* was his marble pillar, his crown of gold, his monument, and the legacy that would outlast him. It was his escape from impermanence, from pain, from a cheating wife and plotting colleagues and an incompetent king and the stark disappearance of any goodness in life.

While still lying like a plank on the floor of his office, he craned his head around to scan the walls of the room. There was a square painting above his desk that showed a lone person falling into a giant volcano, with his whole village watching and cheering below. What Mikalla liked most about this painting was its meaning was purposefully up for interpretation: The falling man could have been a criminal, an idiot, or a noble sacrifice for a purpose that transcended himself.

He was consumed by a gaping loneliness too intense for pictures or stories—he even felt estranged from his own self. He was a spider in the body of a fly—a man crazed who straddled the tightrope between innocent lucidity and predatory insanity. He hungered for his own authentic life force as his mind devoured itself in formless bouts of angst and indignation. Up to that point, he'd believed there was even beauty in ugliness, or at least beautiful derivatives from the most wretched of sources. However, the feeling that engulfed him with needle teeth was too atrocious to become art; there could be nothing beautiful about the void eating away at him. There was nothing nice or attractive or meaningful about the storm overtaking every inch of what he'd thought was his life.

The flame within him he used to illuminate the murals on the walls in the dark labyrinth of life was extinguished. His dead flame left nothing behind but liquid ash, a black ooze that stirred, moaned, and croaked in an endless, howling chasm.

He was, at this point, a shell. An absence of a certain vitality that made him more of a vessel than a man—more of a prophet than a disciple.

***

After closing his eyes for what felt like a minute, the outside window revealed an afternoon sky. He heard footsteps on the wooden floorboards that trickled through the narrow hall and up the stairs to his office. Despite the company approaching, he didn't bother to lift his head off the sweat-crusted parchment balls he called a pillow, let alone stand up.

There was a knock on the door, light and unassuming. "Sir," a small voice said.

"Come in." Mikalla's vocal cords sounded mangled and grated. A short, bony man walked in. His face was old, but his voice was young. "What would you like, Sarsi?"

"Sir, this script is, um…" Sarsi trailed off and started to twist his fingers. Mikalla remained patient and silent, still lying on the floor and looking up at him. "Well, um… when can we get the crew to orient around this new direction?"

"We won't need many of them for this ceremony—just percussionists and vocalists. Send everyone else home. Just supply me with the drum and the props I had them make. This is a special occasion."

"Uhh, are you sure, sir?"

"I'm not going to say it twice, Sarsi. Drum and props, percussionists and vocalists. No one else needs to be there."

"Very well. I'll let them know right away."

Sarsi walked out, and Mikalla stayed lying there, staring even deeper into the void he'd dug for himself. He figured his plan would be a death sentence for some of his crew. But saving those crew members would have meant letting the kingdom die, and his story along with it. Mikalla, with the finality of night, decided those members had to be used. If their lives were taken, that would mean they had saved countless others and—even more than that—the sanctity of expression he needed to invoke.

***

Mikalla wore his wide-hooded brown cloak as he waded through the bustling crowd. On occasion, before ceremonies, he liked to visit the commons and observe the people. He stood in the thick of it and allowed the hum of the capital to swallow him whole. He wore his hood and closed his eyes to stop seeing, then began *to feel*. He listened to the steps of the passersby, to their words, their voices.

He cracked his dry mouth open and sucked in a breath of air. The scent of corn flour, cracked pepper, and the satisfaction of a hard day's salty sweat wafted around. He heard the rhythmic clanking of metal and the strokes of a rowboat drifting by. Gratitude and awe at the balance of it all filled him. It was jumbled, chaotic, disorienting, dizzying, and yet, somehow, balanced all the same. He sometimes felt he *created* that balance, given his platform and influence. It had been there before Mikalla was appointed the Conjurer, and it would be there long after he was gone. But he *was* integral to how that balance thrived during his tenure.

He walked on through a narrow corridor, ducking under hanging tunics and over sleeping dogs. A barefoot child sat against a wall and munched a hunk of bread. He had crumbs on his face and big brown eyes that looked like Coyote's. The boy smiled at him. It was a closed-lipped smile, but a bright one. It was a smile that shone through the eyes, the cheeks, the corners of the lips. Whether it was out of courtesy or compassion for the boy, Mikalla cracked a forced smile back. It was the first time he'd done so in what felt like years. His cheeks were heavy and bloated, and his lips were cracked; when he smiled at the boy, it felt like he was pushing a boulder. He continued down the corridor.

Eventually, the street opened to a pavilion with less clutter and no animals or children. The pavilion tapered toward a towering limestone building with columns in the front and a carved opening that functioned as a doorway. Two guards in black feathers, black linens, and black-striped faces stood on opposite sides of the door. Mikalla pulled his hood even farther down his face. The guards looked at the cloaked Mikalla then at each other. Mikalla felt their eyes but continued on through the massive, open-air entrance.

Inside were more columns and a strong orange light. The ceiling was vaulted, highest at its center, and there were candles everywhere. A bronze statue sat in the middle of the cavernous room. It depicted an eagle with a long beard and a fist raised in the air with a serpent as a necklace. It wore a crown of spikes. Mikalla immediately recognized it as Umbra—a god, a warrior, a character, and one of his many recurring depictions. Mikalla portrayed him as the protector of Idaza and its land, and he was one of his favorite Idazan gods to construct a story around.

Mikalla, as the divinely appointed Conjurer, had the gods passed down to him by his long line of Conjurer predecessors. But the Idazan mythos was less a collection of stories and more so a mound of depictions and interpretations from the root gods of the most ancient times, from further back than Mikalla, or seemingly anyone, cared to know.

Mikalla's job was to take the gods that were given to him, passed down over generations, and make stories with them. He had baselines, history, and a concrete, lengthy mythos of Idazan lore to draw from, yet everything else was still fair game to be created and played with. In a way, Mikalla was the creator, the *prime continuer*, of Idaza's future myths and legendary fables. All that Mikalla spoke at the ceremonies was Idazan canon. The shadows he displayed on the rock were like reflections of the soul of Idaza's past and future. Mikalla showed the continuum, the undulating rhythm that beat at the heart of the kingdom. His job was to either retell stories with the ancient characters and gods or trailblaze new tales with those gods in mind, giving them new life.

To ask whether or not Mikalla believed in the gods was like asking if the sun believed in the rain that fell upon the earth—it didn't matter. Mikalla viewed the gods and the mythos of Idaza as something not to be touched nor understood, too ethereal to do anything but pay reverence. The mystique of the gods excited him, and that childlike fervor was apparent in each one of his stories. But nonetheless, Mikalla couldn't explain the ways of the gods, he could only tell about them. Unlike the high priests of Idaza, who sought to rationalize and covet the secrets of nature, Mikalla was only interested in admiring them from afar, painting pictures with words and shadows about their glory and transcendence.

There were more people toward the room's edges, admiring the many carvings on the flickering, orange-tinted walls. One man stood directly in front of the statue. He gripped a dagger in his left hand and held his right palm out. He began moaning and fidgeting and spitting in what seemed like a trance. After a minute, he stood still and straightened his back.

"Holiest Umbra, may you protect my family and my crop," he said. Then, he inhaled and winced as he sliced his right palm open, so his arm soon ran with a stream of blood. Once his hand began to drip, he knelt and smeared the blood on the ground in front of the statue.

At the sight of this, Mikalla didn't know whether to shake his head, laugh, throw up, or sit back in quiet pride. He pulled his hood down and walked back out into the pavilion.

Chapter 28

King Oro's chair at the ceremony was gold-plated, but he wouldn't be needing it much that night. Instead, he would be standing and pacing and talking with advisers, anxiously anticipating the start of Mikalla's show. The royal booth was the only thing perched above Mikalla during ceremonies, but unlike Mikalla, the king was visible to the crowd. The booth was situated laterally to the projection rock and the sea of commoners. There was something important, if not vital, about the commoners being able to watch the king watching the same display as the rest of Idaza. If the king was to be in the audience, that meant no single person was too good or too busy for the ceremony.

Oro arrived at the royal booth early on the morning of the event. He was greeted by the guards, "Good morning, Your Highness." They knelt.

"Yeah, mm-hmm," the king said as he swooped by them toward his lone chair. Oro's seat overlooked clear skies, empty bleachers, and the sunned projection rock. There was a compulsive spring in his step. When he sat down, he fidgeted and bit his upper lip, shifting his gaze around like a paranoid squirrel.

His mind went the wayward paths of the wind, convulsing, drifting, then storming violently with no warning. The war in his brain was a bloody one with no purpose, no rhyme, no "good side" Oro could root for; it was all a jumbled clump of bodies and horrible yells—the only goal was carnage. He was scared for his friend, for his kingdom. He feared the whims of the crowd and the high-strung nerves of General Jax. And he was mortally afraid for himself. But mostly, what he'd always been told should be at the center of his being—his legacy—was just a *word* to him surrounded by meaningless clichés. At the vital core of his decision-making was a hollowness, a misunderstanding, an anger at the duty handed down to him by his father.

Whatever may happen, whatever Mikalla does, whatever the commoners think at the end of the ceremony, I will not be in control of it. He pictured his father looking down on him, seeing what he'd let this situation become because of inaction. In that fleeting instant, he was clobbered by a fierce, shuddering demon. The demon made his body thirst for an end to the urge and turned the war in his head to a burning pit of hellish groans that stung the ears—the din of a turmoil that it was too late to solve.

He rubbed and slapped his thighs before standing back up and calling to the guards, "Put the seat at a diagonal so it better faces the projection rock. And bring in a few more chairs."

"It will be done, Your Highness."

"Oh, and where's General Jax?"

***

"General, who should take the east entryway?"

"Someone, anyone." He was gruff and short with the soldier. The hum of the previous day's preparation had reached a near frenzy. General Jax scrambled around the stadium, going from soldier to soldier, cohort to cohort, as if preparing for a battle instead of a ceremony. He stomped with tight fists and a clenched jaw, yet he looked on with easy eyes. He had control. He had his men. He had the command of the spear and the tactics to back it up; Jax was a man prepared with a steely focus on a single task. For so much brute determination, he maintained the coldest calm in the stadium—a dim mind that studied well was a content mind. That was Jax: dim and determined.

King Oro stepped up behind the general, who was still preoccupied with the security. "Jax."

The general spun around and knelt at the sound of Oro's voice. "Your Majesty," Jax said, looking at the king's feet.

Oro turned toward all the guards and soldiers in the area. "Gentlemen," the king said, "please give us a moment." At once, everyone cleared out, and the king turned back toward the general. Jax was still on his knee. "Get up, Jax."

"What can I do for Your Highness?" asked the general.

The king grabbed Jax's shoulder and pointed up at his royal booth. "You sit with me tonight," Oro said. He looked into the general's eyes. Oro nudged Jax along with him, and they walked toward the royal booth together. "How many of your men are on the ceremony pyre?"

Jax cleared his throat. "Your Majesty, we have thirty speared soldiers surrounding the ceremonial flame. Everything will be secure. Everything has been planned and discussed. Everyone has been briefed. I have this airtight, Your Majesty."

Oro nodded. "Okay, good. Because it's your head if it isn't." It was a threat to Jax, but the king said it like a routine fact.

And there Oro sat, at the top of the whole winding and churning hierarchy of Idaza, above the farmers and the potters and the bureaucrats and the warriors. From his mountainous view, Oro saw the futility of it all. Yet at the same time, the anxiety of all the outcomes the ceremony could cause rushed through him and choked all of his potential for action. *I am a shred, a victim, a piece of something larger that cannot be stopped. Where are my levers of power—the ones I can pull and not make a mistake? They are either gone or they never existed, but either way, there is no right option for me. I will be hurting people no matter what.*

While the king continued to ruminate, he considered the many paths that could unfold, and not one of them failed to end in the spill of blood, the pain of indecision, or the sucking void of regret. *And for Mikalla, have him do what he likes. At least he'll be forced to make a decision. At least he can choose his own fate, make his own meaning.*

Chapter 29

I t started as a single movement that then rippled throughout the city. On the day of every ceremony, there was a shared understanding among all the kingdom's people. No matter what they ate earlier that day or who they happened to pass by in the streets, there was a heavy air of predestination that loomed in the back of each and every one of the commoners' minds. All roads led back to the ceremony. All minds were bent and strung to the same stories. Every minuscule commoner was but a fragment within the colossal Idazan mosaic.

The first person left her home and started toward the stadium. She had a tan tunic that stretched to her ankles and long, sleek black hair. Her eyes were the color of coffee beans, and she had a small mouth and a tight jaw. Her sandals clopped on the street outside, alerting her neighbors. Then, another neighbor saw her walking. There was soon a group of Idazans in the street, all striding and stomping together. Steadily, more and more neighbors took notice and followed. The cluster grew too big and flooded the whole route with people. From a bird's eye view, they looked like a single surge of water coming down a pipe, or ants awash in an uncontrollable tide. It was the Idazan people—the colossus of commoners coalesced.

The commoners hummed and vibrated through the many streets. They were frenzied, but the state hoped they were frenzied in the *right* way.

The commoners kept themselves in check as the soldiers could only do so much with a mass that large. This was why they needed their shepherd. This was why they needed their sweet stories to give them peace, to create blissful camaraderie in their hearts. The giant shadow puppets connected them. They were united in the name of the king, but *not* because of him. It was the shadows that bound them. It was because of their shepherd that they so wanted to be herded.

***

Earlier during the day of the ceremony, Jani and Kitan had sat in the council chamber at the palace shortly after King Oro left for the stadium.

"Jani, I understand your allegiance is to the kingdom, and that is *most* commendable," Kitan said, putting his hand to his chest and closing his eyes. "But with that said, Mikalla must have done something fairly severe to warrant this kind of treatment from you, no? After all, he is your husband."

Jani paused for a while and glanced at the vaulted cone of a ceiling above them. She was still and stiff. "No, not really."

Kitan raised his eyebrows. "Not at all?"

"Not overtly, no."

Kitan leaned close to her, his eyes slits. His tongue looked pronged and snake-like when it lashed. "What about *co*vertly?"

Jani swallowed. Then she took another pause. "He's... weak."

Kitan leaned his head back and squinted, as if surprised by the answer. "And what do you mean by that?"

"I... it's really nothing. You know him; you tell me." It was difficult from her fixed position to tell her heart was pounding.

"Well," Kitan started, "I've always thought he was rather *strong*, actually."

Jani just shook her head and huffed to herself. Kitan hung onto every wobble, flick, smirk, and swipe of her brow with still, interested eyes. "He never stands up for himself. Sometimes, it's like he doesn't even *have* a self."

Kitan smiled and tilted his head up so his narrow nostrils were visible to Jani. "Hm. I see." Kitan shrouded his prodding with dramatic changes in his tone. His pitch went up. "And what would you, then, consider to be *your* self?"

Jani crossed her arms and turned away. "My self and my allegiance and all of my actions," she said, bobbing her head to the rhythm of her words, "are for the king."

"Right. And so, that's what you're proud of?"

Jani torqued her head like it had been pulled with a rope. Every movement of her fingers and arms looked mechanical and planned. "Idaza is my only pride."

"You know, Jani, you are one of the last true nobles left."

"I know."

"Your blood and your character are greater than anyone else around us. You honestly should have been placed in my position instead of me."

Jani was taken aback by Kitan's modesty. She felt his guard slip and melt away. To her, Kitan had exposed his soft underbelly, and she was ready to plunge.

"Really?" She scrunched her face, selling disbelief. "What makes you say that?"

Kitan twiddled his thumbs. He looked like an embarrassed child—hunched and despondent. "Jani, I care too much." He expelled air from his mouth loudly. "I'm too interested in hearsay and the drama of it all. I care too much about people. I'm not as *focused* as you." Kitan looked her directly in the eyes.

A glare that would have turned anybody else to stone made Jani blush. "Secretary, you do a fine job as it is. I am perfectly content where I am."

Kitan pushed his chair back and stood up. "Do you mind? I need to stretch my legs."

"Not at all."

Kitan, upright and stretched, now looked out the window at the Idazan horizon. His back was to Jani, and so were his intentions. "Jani, I'm going to be frank when I say this: You are the most talented person in the government. We need you now more than ever. With all this strife, all this uncertainty—you are the *rock*."

"Thank you, Mister Secretary. I've always known you to be honorable. You're being modest."

"But Jani, there's one thing."

"Yes?"

"You know Mikalla has been disobedient. You were the one who unearthed his disloyalty to the state."

"Yes."

"And yet," Kitan said, still facing the window away from Jani. A smirk slithered onto his face, and he held his arm at a right angle as if giving a speech. "I still sense that you're attached to him."

"That's ridiculous!" She scratched her fingers on the seat's cushion. "What makes you say that?"

"He's the father of your child, Jani. Please don't blame yourself. You have nothing to be ashamed of."

"Kitan, he's an enemy of the state and deserves to be ostracized, *especially* by me!"

"So." Kitan turned around so he could drink in Jani's every facial movement. He studied her with care. "Then you'd be fine if he died?" Pleasantry left him like a ghastly demon fleeing a successful exorcism. He was stoic, focused, and calm.

Jani gulped and sat back down with her eyes locked on the tabletop map. She rubbed her face up and down with her now-sweaty palms. Her cheeks and eyelids stretched and wrinkled.

She thought back to simpler times, when she didn't have to calculate everything she said and did—when everybody was in their rightful place. She thought of Mikalla, and the golden glint of his face sparked a memory…

The baby was born healthy. Everything about him sparkled even more than the hooped bracelets Jani wore. The day prior, the many medics and priests on the scene that gathered around Coyote's birth were adamant about his good looks and his destiny as a great noble among Idazans everywhere. Jani, of course, knew this instinctually. After all, the baby was from her.

She was alone now with Coyote, who was babbling and cooing and looking up at Jani with his big, deep eyes. She looked out at the expansive living room. It had no people in it. Not her mother and father meeting their newest grandchild, nor any one of her slew of siblings meeting their brown-eyed, fuzzy-haired new nephew. She had everything, but at the same time, she had no one.

She heard Coyote's mumbling echo throughout her cavernous house. She looked down at her child and told herself she didn't need her family. She had Coyote, and that was all. That was her family. She said it was okay. She told the baby she would never forsake him, that she would always love him. She whispered to Coyote that she didn't need anyone else, but she was good at lying to herself; lying helped the tears streaming down her face dissipate a little faster. At least the tears kept her company. At least the tears were there when she was feeling lonely and sad.

Just then, she heard footsteps in the home's entrance. Her head whipped back to face the noise. "Mom? Dad? Here's your new grandson!" But it was Mikalla.

"They still haven't shown up?" Mikalla asked, sounding concerned. He got closer and noticed the tears streaming down her face. He saw the despair in her eyes, the precipice she teetered

so daringly upon. He pulled out an object from behind his back. It was his painting. He nestled beside Jani and Coyote, touching foreheads with Jani and wiping her tears away with his thumb. He slowly kissed her then his son's forehead. "Look what I made for you, baby."

The painting was a portrait of the three of them, smiling and cuddling and happy. They stood tall and straight, and their smiles were kind and honest. Mikalla stroked Jani's chin and looked her in the eyes. "We're all we need, Jani. I love you."

And just as soon as they came, Mikalla made Jani's tears go away, back down to the simmering depths of her gut, not to resurface for a long time.

Jani came back to Kitan. "An enemy of the state is an enemy of mine," she said hurriedly, twitching as she spoke. Her brow furrowed, and she looked away.

Kitan nodded slowly and stroked his chin. He looked out at the horizon. "Let's hope he stays on script, then."

Chapter 30

On his way to the ceremony, Kitan delved into his world of unconscious musings—his deep being filled with patterns, schematics, and calculations. He saw the waves underneath the static objects. Kitan walked outside and gazed at the forest surrounding his house, thick and layered with trees—he felt the network of their roots, their interdependence, and admired how it all worked, how each fruit and acorn provided sustenance. He considered the math behind the schematic cycle, beneath the mad, fruitless flow of it all.

Kitan strode on through the forest, and from up above, he saw the crowds filtering through corridors and canals, squeezing tight as they streamed toward the stadium. Just like the forest, he thought of the many people as sustenance flowing through the roots of the city. As the lifeblood of the city, he knew the people had to be directed. That bloodstream had to filter somewhere vital, or else the body of the city would end up bleeding, or worse yet, wilting into a bottomless decay. Kitan shuddered at the prospect of decay, at the idea of a leaf that has to fall; in Kitan's mind, not every leaf had to fall and not every tree had to die—the roots could be manipulated to enable life to continue.

He glared down at the city streets filled with people all marching in one direction. And deep in his writhing gut, he knew Mikalla was their heart, their beating rhythm, pulsing for some life that mistook futility for beauty.

Mikalla was the ignorant pied piper, the palpitating heartbeat of the city that needed to be replaced. Kitan didn't quite know how to do that, but with a surgical hand, he'd have to try. As he observed the canals and corridors flowing with people, he saw their compulsivity, their hive mind destined for obligation, meant to be told what to do. He scorned them but loved the process. However, with every one of his frail steps, the threat of Mikalla's flickering shadow only loomed larger. His thin grip on the controls, the handle he'd thought he held firm, felt shaky in his palm. *I cannot leave this up to Mikalla. This situation is too delicate—these people are held too captive—to be left in his childish hands.* Spears and schemes floated through Kitan's mind. As this conflict built up inside, his schemes and calculations became muddled, jumbled, desperate. Kitan was nervous.

Without a plan, Kitan itched. He couldn't stay still. The swirling crowds below him built into a frenzy as the noise became too loud. In the face of the chaos, he was forced to react, not strike. There was nothing to be proactive about, there was only barren land—dry and used, frenzied and confused. Mikalla was the block in his head. *Jani will go along with whatever.* But pesky questions kept springing up, and he couldn't shake their eerie persistence: *What will Mikalla do? What is Mikalla thinking? This is my fault! I left too much power in his hands, and now look at me. I never get nervous, and yet, here I am. I should have done better, I should have pushed Oro harder, I should have fired that weakling Zac... No one besides me is effective at all, yet I failed my job of being one hundred percent certain of the outcome.*

Kitan was often his own greatest opponent, and he seemed to have defeated himself on his walk to the stadium. His spiral weighed on him, but he wouldn't forego his swiftness of action; no, Kitan was ready for war and blood. In fact, to Kitan, blood was the lubricant, the gas, the oil—it was the light in a crowded forest, the solution to an opaque problem.

There will be blood. There must be blood. Kitan trembled. *Blood is the answer because that's all I've been left with.*

Chapter 31

For every ceremony, Mikalla was painted and adorned with feathers and beads. It was less of an outfit and more of a uniform. To be the Conjurer, he thought it most appropriate to dress until he could no longer recognize himself. Looking into the mirror, though, he could not escape the eyes glaring back at him. No matter how many ornaments or jewels he put on his skin, he couldn't cover himself enough. When he looked in the mirror, he saw an abyss gaze back at him and swallow him whole. In his gaze, he felt an intimate proximity to death. Maybe he was death itself. Maybe he looked at his appearance and realized it was not him that mattered, but his message. He was a prophet, a vessel.

When his eyes looked back at him in the mirror, he felt the full extent of the futility of who he was.

He felt the parameters he'd always been bound by. The weight of his lifelong constriction flashed inside him all at once.

He felt himself poke through the veneer that was his duty, the duty that long kept him sheathed as a tool and not as a being.

Quietly and stiffly, in the torchlight of the dingy studio bathroom, he became enraged. It built up in him like slow, viscous magma. His rage drew out what he had suppressed his whole life, like a blue force field emanating from his chest. He continued to swing his head around, and every time he saw an object or a wall, he felt the gravity of the rules. The whole of his past flashed through his eyes through the lens of his constraints. The people and their expectations did not feed Mikalla; they were bent only on keeping him in line long enough to serve Idaza and its growth. Every new construction in Idaza was another limitation, and every new position was a different shackle to bear.

Mikalla took a knife from a cabinet and sliced both of his cheeks with slow strokes, leaving thin slices.

He had no more shackles.

The blood ran down his face. He had no more burdens.

He smashed the mirror in front of him. He had no more appearances.

The shards stung like many wasps. He had no more worries.

He looked at his ruined, bloody makeup then down at his bruised and lacerated hand. He stared at himself, and after a while, his grimace melted into laughter. He grinned and giggled. The joy from his chuckles almost made him want to live again.

He was not Mikalla—he was the Conjurer, as he had always truly been.

***

Slowly, the stadium filled—at first, it was a trickle, but it soon became a flood. The sun bowed at its peak one last time before vacating its blue stage, leaving behind streaks of purple and orange. As the light waned over Mount Chuxat, the energy of the arena steadily picked up. What was initially a hum of eager commoners became a concentrated beam. Under the speckled sky, a great hammer of attention, influence, and *power* was being forged. The sea of commoners below was a tremorous mountain as powerful as nature itself—and in a way, it *was* nature, in all of its frenzied ugliness and seismic proportion.

Oro sat in his booth, looking down at it all. He was surrounded by his elite coterie, as usual—Jani, Coozma, Jax, Kitan, Zac, and others. Three priests stood in the back of the booth, and a few more faceless, gilded nobles sat laterally to the king.

The air grew colder and heavier, like a chilled purple blanket descending on the masses. Its gravity sucked Oro in. The weight of the anticipation tightened his neck and jaw. From behind, he looked like a shadow superimposed on the arena. His line of sight fell across the sea of commoners and toward the projection rock. The whole of the kingdom was below him.

Idaza wasn't defined by its huts or canals or statues or crops. Idaza was what it was because of the arena right in front of Oro— the stories it told and the people who watched them.

At that moment, King Oro overlooked his kingdom, but he was not part of it. He ran it, but he did not live in it, nor did he engage with it. It was during the ceremonies when, despite being able to see every citizen, he felt most detached from his public— if it was even *his* to begin with.

"Your Majesty, look." General Jax, with his battle-hardened hawk eyes, spotted a figure walking toward the platform above the stadium seating. He pointed at a silhouette that sauntered under the forming stars—slow, indignant.

"Finally," said King Oro. He was hunched over, squinting and fixated on the shadowy figure in the distance, but he talked like he was uninterested. "He's here."

The royal booth became silent, still, and watchful.

Chapter 32

Mikalla took off his robe and threw it on the cold, stony ground as he walked toward the platform. He took his time with each step. The blood that had gushed down his cheeks had since dried and hardened in the wind of the night. His crew turned around and gawked at the man they once knew— emaciated, bloody, stone-faced. They made way for him as he wedged through, not acknowledging anyone or anything except for his next step.

"Cymbals, ready." The frigid gusts of the heights amplified Mikalla's near-whisper into a booming command. With every swipe of his arm or subtle finger flick, the wind seemed to extend and lash out with his movements. The percussionists scrambled like lost baby chicks to their places, and the vocalists frantically assembled. The same grim look overtook the faces of each and every one of his crew members: an acute bewilderment and a primal kind of fear, something trembling in wait, terrified of what the future held. They were wobbly and mortified, shaken to the core. It was an eternal fear—not of death as a finality but death as an entryway into unending, black torture. Whether by the state or by society or by all their peers and families growing up, it was a deep-seated fear that Mikalla was now tearing out of them. He held the black virus in front of their faces for all of them to see.

The trembling crew was in position. There was something about Mikalla's overt calmness that terrified and shocked them; they had snakes in their spines, writhing and rattling their song of angst. Everything about their week of preparation was wrong and broken. They had no cadence, nothing but a bare-bones script they'd practiced once. They had nothing to hold onto except for drumsticks and the whims of their leader's commands, who seemed unhinged and catatonic. He was a skeletal zombie. But he was the only one in the kingdom who wasn't anticipating anything—who wasn't looking forward, but rather lived in that cold, present moment. He stood above all with still breath and large, monstrous pupils like hungry voids.

He was the one who was anticipated.

At that specific moment, no amount of gold, spears, or coercion could have plucked him from the middle of the vortex. He *was* the vortex.

"Vocals, ready." Mikalla was somber and still. His voice was scratched and strained—as striking as the sound of the wind itself. It was like listening to the very rhythm of nature in all of its terror, strife, and suffering.

"Light the flame." Mikalla looked directly at the pyre as it transformed into a furiously dancing orange behemoth. Its unmistakable light emanated throughout the arena. The crowd bellowed and roared at the onset of the light. They were maddened by it. The stars and moon surrounding the open-air arena now paled in comparison to the vigor of the ceremonial flame.

Every flicker of the dancing orange terror from above made the sea of commoners look like they moved with it, yet they were all still. They were frozen by the rigidity of the packed bleachers—captive and vulnerable. Together, they were a wave and a consolidated mass too forcible to be quelled. Together, they were the reason for everything in Idaza—they *were* Idaza. But apart, individually, each commoner was constrained by the others surrounding them. Under the gaze of Mikalla, they were crammed in by those to the left and right and above and below them.

Mikalla was the only one close enough to feel the heat of the pyre. His paint dripped and ran, and the thin scabs on his face opened back up. He was barely human—either that, or all too human. He spanned his arms out as wide as they could go. He let the energy of the fire flow through him, *consume* him.

He looked up at the sky, closed his eyes, and took a breath.

***

"What is he doing?" Jani muttered. She squinted and leaned in. Her shoulders hunched up to her neck.

"Patience, Jani," Kitan said. He sat back in his cushioned chair in the royal booth and crossed one leg over the other. "He has the business end of the spear as his incentive. He'll be fine."

King Oro slugged from his goblet. "The revised script was good. All he has to do now is follow it."

***

Mikalla walked to the edge of the platform. He saw the people. If they had each been mindless drones, Mikalla wouldn't have cared for their attention at all. He wouldn't have cared about cultivating the anticipation; he wouldn't have cared to grip them as captive consumers. It was their humanity—their flesh, their pain, the nutrients that filtered through their vital veins and fed their eyes and hearts—that comprised their lives, which gave life to the deathly myths told and passed down.

The flame behind him cast his colossal shadow onto the projection rock. His hands were still outstretched.

The first cymbal clanged. The metal shattered through the glass ruckus of the crowd. The next cymbal clanged. Then the next. There was a succession of them, moving like a wave through the air and enveloping any other sound that dared try and compete in the arena. Then, the gong struck. It blanketed even the cymbals.

The drums rolled like thunder. The rumble shook the stadium, and the children in the crowd covered their ears. The vocalists made a seamless entrance into the soundscape. It was roaring and smooth and operatic. The hundreds of thousands of people now looked like tendrils of the same organism, bobbing and gyrating in a wide-eyed trance.

The chorus went on.

"Here we go," King Oro said. He leaned forward and bit his bottom lip with his yellowed front teeth.

Mikalla walked out along the platform in front of the flame. It burned and burped and spat out coals the size of hot daggers. Mikalla lifted his arms yet higher. The shadow towered over the rest. On the projection rock, Mikalla's silhouette was defined and distorted. It cavorted and stayed still. It smiled and cried. It leaned and swayed like a collapsing tower that never fell.

The paint and blood that ran down his body were one and the same. He lowered one hand and fisted his other. He inhaled deeply and doubled the size of his chest. The drums thumped like a giant racing heartbeat. The chorus cried out just to be heard. The cymbals rang. It was both cacophonous and coordinated—it made ears bleed and vibrate in pleasure.

Then, the gong rang again. A sanitizing silence washed over the instruments, the chorus, and the crowd. The crickets ceased their chirping, the scorpions stopped traipsing, and the goats stood at attention. Even the chatter from the royal booth ceased for a moment.

In a way, the silence was louder than the tune before it, but it was certainly more peaceful. Then, Mikalla, like a mallet through glass, shattered the stillness of the kingdom. He spat as he shrieked from the top of the arena.

"My people," Mikalla said, his voice strained even at his first words, "live your own stories. Tell your *own* stories. Form your *own* images. For your own story is all you have!"

The cold wind of the night was a mouthpiece. It took Mikalla's guttural yells and delivered them to every set of ears in the arena's bleachers. It made Mikalla's screeching feel more like a strong whisper in the ears of each and every individual—like padded, reassuring vibrations.

***

The whispers of the night wind reached the royal booth, but there, Mikalla's rhetoric fell upon closed ears. Instead, they talked over it.

"This is off script," Oro said, treating his own hand like a scrumptious leg of lamb. His back was hunched, and his eyes were wide.

The rest of the nobles squirmed and fussed.

General Jax stood up so quickly, his chair fell. "Your Majesty, my men are ready—"

"Yes, yes, I know."

"Just say the word." Jax balled his hands into sweaty, iron fists. He stood from the royal booth with his calves flexed, as if he could pounce from the balcony right onto the Conjurer's platform. "I knew it. I knew he'd do this!" Jax gritted his teeth, and his jaw trembled.

The king shot up to face Jax. His brow was a sweat gutter as he sucked his lips into his mouth. "Hold on." Oro stuck his bearish arm out as if to contain Jax. "Just hold on!"

"He's off the script, Oro. There's nothing we can do!"

"Just shut up!"

"Your Majesty, he's right," Kitan said. The secretary got up and stood in between the king and the general.

Oro threw his goblet against the stone ground of the balcony and kicked another at a guard. Wine sprayed everywhere until the royal booth smelled like Oro's breath.

Oro stomped up to Secretary Kitan. He shoved his meaty index finger right under the gaunt secretary's nose. "Give him a moment."

***

The arena was encased in the Conjurer's shadow. It swayed, and they swayed. The shadow and the commoners tangoed under the majesty of the stars, the greatness of the ceremonial flame, and the paranoid eye of the royal booth.

Somehow, the Conjurer both entranced and enlightened the commoners, trapping them and freeing them.

Mikalla spoke. It was as if the whole world was watching. In a way, it was. Latched onto the tip of his flicking tongue was the gravity of centuries past and the generations of the future, all clinging to his lone story that night; then and there was the Conjurer, architecting the future by means of the past.

"There once lived a healthy seed. Once it fell to the rich soil, it was ready to grow, expand, and actualize itself even past the image of its forefathers. But my people," the Conjurer's tone became ominous, flipped to a looming violence that sharpened his booming words, "our baby seed, our hero, lay in a valley of treachery, of *death*!"

The stadium whipped into a frenzy. There was a strong wind from the gasps of the countless Idazans. The Conjurer cracked a smile at their reaction, at their delicious fear.

He knew he had them hooked.

"Yes, in this treacherous soil were thieves, great fanged creatures, worms, snakes, varmints, crawlers, competitors, and *killers*!" Mikalla screamed that last word like it came from his soul and not his mouth. The crowd was electrified, static with awe. "There was not one among them that wished for the seed to grow, to flourish and become itself."

***

General Jax had to be held back by the guards. He tried to rush out of the royal booth to give the word, and Oro was angered by his impulsivity—unauthorized and unabashed. "*I* give the *word*," the king growled through his teeth. Now restrained by the guards, Jax fell to his knees and hyperventilated on the ground. His chest puffed, and he spat at their feet.

Jax sputtered on with sweaty strands of hair hanging over his crazed eyes. "He's talking about some *seed*! *Off script*! We kill him—now! We should have seen this coming. Kill him! These are—"

Oro cut him off, this time in a soft voice. He was in a trance, a solemn state of reverie; he didn't want to have to do this. He thought he had better control than this, but then again, he knew better. His dissidents were fighting opposing dissenters, and the war in his head raged as loudly as the chaos in the stadium. Softly, he commanded, "Guards, remove his head."

Jax said nothing, but his eyes rolled with terror. One of the men gave a ghostlike strike with a phantom blade at Jax's neck. With a few deliberate swipes, it toppled off the general's broad shoulders.

Jax's blood mixed with the wine and covered the whole royal booth in a puddle of rich, marbled red. Jax's larynx flopped onto the floor to reveal his detached vocal cords. What were pure, pearly white a moment ago were now soaked in the blood of the grape and Jax's own gore—they were vocal cords that had attempted to save the order of the kingdom while also dismaying the highest position in the land. It was the gravity of power that ripped the general apart, and all the blade did was finish the job.

Jani and Kitan looked at each other with their mouths open. The only sound from the royal booth was now the fluid from Jax's neck bubbling into a burgundy stew and the scrape of obsidian being sheathed. The general's now-dead eyes revealed a truth: Jax may have commanded the spears, but Oro controlled them—he always had. The king walked to the edge of the balcony, soaking his feet with each step, and grimaced at the ceremony and its proceedings.

Oro looked out and did not see the great, spellbinding caster of narrative whimsy. He did not see a public servant, nor a master artist performing his craft. He saw a friend. He saw the only person in the kingdom, let alone the nobility, who recognized the king's heart also pumped blood like the rest, that his primal mind choked with anxiety from time to time, and his fleshy feet swelled from standing too much; he was all too human.

He saw Mikalla, not the Conjurer. Mikalla had always treated him not as the king, but exactly, *beautifully*, normally like a person. And now, his best friend was his greatest roadblock.

***

"At first," the Conjurer bellowed, "it was the snake who slithered by the seed. It did not hunger for the seed but was instead crafty and bored." A writhing figure slithered onto the projection rock—fanged, scaled, a restless, resentful shadow. "The snake hissed and mocked the seed: 'You're the infant of what I've already become. Lesser. You're tiny, and you can't even slither. You're a failure. You'll never be able to escape the hawks nor the crows.' The seed tried to scramble but couldn't. It tried to slither desperately but couldn't. It tried to do the snake's work out of fear, anguished at the idea of a violent death."

Mikalla's voice grew louder, deeper, and scratchier. His words stilled the commoners and snatched the air from the arena. Everything that was not Mikalla's voice became an absence—a void consumed by the vacuum of space and consciousness. "Then along came the hawk—proud, bold, and fast." Blistering across the projection rock was a shooting figure, flashing by in a frayed mania then resolutely settling into its upright shape. "The seed began to quiver as winged death looked into its very soul!"

The stars burned while the stadium erupted with nauseous gasps and hurling yelps.

"'Are you going to eat me?' the seed asked. 'No! You're my prey's prey, too weak for me. You're a pathetic pebble—not mighty enough to feed my likeness.' And with that, the seed grew fiery with anger, bitter at the world that birthed it as such a worthless little speck. It turned its anger in on itself. It writhed, cursing its own bitter being. For it did not know what it was, the power it held, full of fear and anger!"

***

Oro shuddered. He scratched his thighs and scalp, but stayed in place with soaked red feet, his tone rough. "What is he doing?" The king's eyes grew sad, and his entire demeanor was laced with defeat. He withdrew so heavily from the circumstances that his body and face and frame were just parts of a ghostly shell.

Kitan shot up at once. He splashed and barreled toward the king with palms open. "Your Majesty, he's ruining everything—you need to do something."

"I know," Oro said.

"It's in *your* hands now."

"Secretary," the king started, "that was never my audience. The hearts of the commoners never belonged to the kingdom." King Oro thrust his index finger at the projection rock—at the towering absence of light that was Mikalla's silhouette. "They belonged to him."

Kitan contorted and twitched. "Yes, that may be the case, but I—*we* need you to make the call here, Your Majesty. I need to know your plan." He dripped with sweat. His characteristic calm was replaced with a shivering urgency.

"I know."

"He's ruining everything. Right now!"

King Oro turned back toward the guards and slipped out a command. "Wine. More… please."

Jani got up and stood right alongside Secretary Kitan. In the light of the ceremonial flame, her face looked puffy and leathery. "Oro, the farmland. Idaza needs this. It needs you."

King Oro walked by Jani and sat back down in his seat to face the ceremony. He looked down at the captive sea of commoners. His breaths were silent, his gaze was steady, and his eyes were hollow.

The king looked away from her, from them, from it all. "I need this, too, Jani."

***

The ceremonial flame grew redder and hotter. It singed the sky above and illuminated the countless flickering, washed-out faces. There was a pleading vulnerability lacing the Conjurer's voice that the audience latched onto. They hung onto every word and bounced lightly to the rhythm of his coarse speech, his searing story, the one that could free them.

"The seed sat there, trembling from the snake and bitterly ashamed from the hawk. The seed, in its short life, had hated itself and others. Then, the seed matured a bit. It grew roots that it scorned, a web of tinged, winding, and frayed spindles. The seed loathed its natural roots; it didn't understand its own nature. It said, 'If I could have been made even more unsightly, even less fit, then it has been done with these appendages!' The seed was a mess, lying in a grave of its own making. Then, a spider came along and saw the roots of the seed spread out like spindly legs. The passing spider mistook the seed for another spider."

On the projection rock was a violent mess of legs and pincers and a jumble of furious eyes. "It first tried to gobble the seed, but to no avail—for the seed's shell was too tough. The spider said, 'Why do you have so many legs?'

"To which the seed replied, 'Because I am a monster, a failed worm.'

"The spider said, 'No, you're a terrific spider. You're no worm at all. In fact, your essence is the greatest among our kind—we will worship you, the hard head with many legs!'

"And they did. For weeks, spiders came from far and wide to pay homage to the many-legged spider, crowds of them chanting its praise. The seed was finally happy. It thought it found a home, a niche, a pedestal. That is, until its roots grew too fat and it popped its first infantile sprout with a leaf and a stalk. The spiders did not understand why it looked this way, why it grew this way. It confused them and upset them: 'That's no spider!' they yelled at the sprout.

"The thousands of gathering spiders demanded an answer— they yelled and hissed at the traitor, the sprout, the failed spider gone wrong like some alien imposter. Then, they chomped at the sprout, left it in tatters, and covered it in a thick mound of impenetrable webs—they attacked it with the vigor of an angry mob betrayed. The sprout suffocated under the endless silk, not knowing which way was up or even what it was, what it was meant to be. It was left alone and battered, fatigued from being tossed and forgotten; it had been scorned too many times. Yet, its roots continued to grow. They absorbed more minerals, more vital nutrients that helped it thrive; the sprout got taller and burst out of its cobweb prison. It gained strength despite its loneliness and confusion. And still, my people, our hero grew!"

***

"Oro! This is ridiculous! What about Chihopo? What about the taxes? What about uniting the kingdom under this one cause?" Jani looked out at the giant shadow projection, its shapes and quivering sights shifting like impossible images.

Oro slugged the rest of his gold goblet, tilted it skyward, and licked the inside clean. His eyes squinted, and he began to nod off. Before his head could reach the back of his chair, he coughed and vomited violently. The green and orange soup of bile and wine poured—it ran down his own face and tunic then spilled onto the booth's puddled floor and inside the neck, head, and still open eyes of General Jax.

King Oro lay in his mess, eyes rolled back into purple oblivion. His mouth opened into an endless chasm, nothingness. He was nothing, and his kingdom was no longer a kingdom.

A growl exploded out of Kitan as he began yelling at the guards. "Kill him! Kill him now! Go!"

The guard took one look at the incapacitated king then signaled to a cohort of soldiers, who surrounded the ceremony crew on the other side of the arena. One of the warriors gave a distinct nod before they all lifted their spears. The crew on the platform was then charged by the soldiers.

Away from the platform, the crew of drummers and singers were picked off. The silver tips of the spears sank into their chests and eyes, leaving a bloodied pile of bodies. All they could do to struggle was put up their hands and back into the wall. It was the spear tip that drove them back, that maintained their jobs and possessions, and that ultimately ended their lives.

The ceremonial flame, unceasing and indiscriminate, lit the pile of bodies with a red and orange glow. What was then just a lump of dead flesh flickered in the blaze. The clumped red blood and limp arms glistened and waved.

Cast on the projection rock was a being larger than life itself. The Conjurer—he was the whole symphony without the need for strings nor percussion nor woodwind nor brass. His voice became the wind itself; at that impending hour, standing on the precipice of everything, he was most liberated. People have a fascination with beings of the greatest heights, and the Conjurer represented just that.

"And so, the sprout grew into a sapling; it became harder, tougher, taller. It looked down at the ground from which it came and shuddered, and then it looked up at the sky to where it was going and shuddered. It was alien to itself, its bark hated its leaves, and its branches hated its wretched, swollen roots. And, my people, where did all this hatred come from? From others, it came! From creepers, crawlers, killers, and demons that never needed it anyway!" The hairs on Mikalla's neck stood up. He trembled for the last time and gazed down at the commoners. They looked like the many gangly feelers of a whispering anemone. "And so," Mikalla went on, "the sapling, filled with rage, hating all directions it came from and could go, rejected the ground and its body that grew from it. It forced its nutrients out; it scorned its uncertain future and the pain that it wrought. And, my people of Idaza, the sapling wilted. It wilted from the horrors of the snake and the vicious doubts of the hawk; it wilted from the abandonment of its spider family that once sang its praise."

The projection rock then depicted more than one person—a hoard of men trampling in the background. It was a visual circus. The whole sea of commoners gasped at the same time.

"But mostly, my people, our sapling died by believing the stories it was told. A seed cannot grow if in its heart it believes it's a pebble. My people, you are seeds, not pebbles nor worms! Be wary of every story you are told, every command you receive, every threat that is cast upon you! For you are a seed; do not be afraid to grow."

Mikalla's last syllable fizzled out. The shadows on the projection rock were now a mess—a shadowy liquid seemed to run out of the Conjurer's head, and a line went through his torso at an angle. The hoard of men in the background got larger and became a jumble of arms and violent thrusts. Then, after a cacophonous moment, the only sound in the whole arena and kingdom was the crackle of the ceremonial flame. It got a little dimmer. The great hammer of attention dropped to the ground and rusted over.

Jani and Kitan's faces eased up, and Oro stopped snoring. The soldiers in front of the ceremonial flame stood still and tucked their spears in like the bashful tails of well-fed dogs. Even the flame paid reverence to the moment and quieted its crackling.

Shy droplets of blood dripped down to the arena. The audience turned their attention back to the platform overhead, where the blood leaked. Every red drop took its gloating time in the air before finally slapping the puddle below. Soon, what had been a sad sprinkler became a rivulet, then a small, glistening burgundy stream. Then, a white and blue body followed. Just like the drops of blood, the body took its time in the air, falling from the platform and into the crowd.

The only eyes in the entire kingdom not affixed to the falling corpse were King Oro's. Yes, he was covered in vomit, and his body was inflamed from the toxic alcohol, but he was safe and happy in his rippling dreamscape, away from the death of his friend and the chaos in his own kingdom. Even in death, Mikalla had the delicious attention of Idaza in his grasp, except his cold hands could no longer keep a tight grip.

After free falling, Mikalla's body hit the ground with a skeletal thud. His face was slashed and mangled, but his razor jawline was still intact. A gentle smile could be discerned behind the dried blood and mountainous bruises littering his face.

A gust of wind overcame the arena, and the flame of Idaza went out. There were no more shadows cast in the dark of the night, and no more myths created. The great deities that once lived in the hearts and minds of the kingdom perished that night, along with the body of the Conjurer who made them.

AUTHOR BIO

Nick Oliveri is an author who treasures the unique potential behind every person's story and values sharing those tales with the world. Skilled at crafting sentences that bring his characters and their narratives to life, he is passionate about the beauty the written word has to offer. *The Conjurer* is Nick's breakout novel and embodies his love of storytelling and the power our voices possess.

Nick was the co-founder of Impact Snacks, a sustainable snacking company dedicated to the onset of the circular economy for consumers and businesses alike. Originally from Massachusetts, Nick currently resides in San Luis Obispo, CA, and loves wine, hockey, surfing, philosophy, art, and of course, reading and writing. Nick has more novels in the works, so keep an eye out for his future writings.

Made in the USA
Middletown, DE
22 December 2021

55149975R00116